GLAS NEW RUSSIAN WRITING

contemporary Russian literature
in English translation

Volume 42

Alexander Pokrovsky

SEA STORIES

Alexander Terekhov

ARMY STORIES

glas
MOSCOW

glas
MOSCOW

GLAS PUBLISHERS
tel./fax: +7(495)441-9157
perova@glas.msk.su
www.russianpress.com/glas

Edited by Natasha Perova and Joanne Turnbull
Camera-ready copy by Tatiana Shaposhnikova
Front cover collage: photographs by Arkady Babchenko

DISTRIBUTION

in **North America**
NORTHWESTERN UNIVERSITY PRESS
CHICAGO DISTRIBUTION CENTER
tel: 1-800-621-2736 or (773) 702-7000
fax: 1-800-621-8476 or (773) 702-7212
pubnet@202-5280
www.nupress.northwestern.edu

in the **UK**
INPRESS LIMITED
tel: 020 8832 7464; fax: 020 8832 7465
mail1@inpressbooks.co.uk
www.inpressbooks.co.uk

Within **Russia** Glas is distributed by
JUPITER-IMPEX
www.jupiters.ru
see also www.ozon.ru; www.bolero.ru

ISBN 978-5-7172-0079-0

CONTENTS

THE HARSH MALE WORLD OF THE ARMY

"The Russian army is now in shambles, a psychological wreck, a material ruin. *Dedovshchina*, the sadistic, often fatal, hazing of recruits, is ubiquitous: soldiers are routinely humiliated and tortured by their commanders, beaten with sticks, anything at hand. Every year thousands are wounded and hundreds are killed or commit suicide, thousands more go AWOL as a result of the abuse… For many officers life has been so leached of a sense of mission and pride that they destroy themselves with drink; their salaries are so low that they ease into a life of corruption, petty or grand." – David Remnick, "Post-imperial Blues" (*The New Yorker*)

These near-documentary pieces by Alexander Pokrovsky and Alexander Terekhov provide vivid illustrations to the above observation. They have been only slightly fictionalized for the sake of readability. Pokrovsky and Terekhov both vouch for their complete veracity and insist that things have got even worse since the mid-1990s when they were first published. Cruel treatment, constant hunger, lack of sleep, and the general senselessness of army training are the recurrent themes of these stories (Terekhov is particularly explicit on the subject.)

The phenomenon of *dedovshchina* first became public knowledge only in the late 1980s though it had been acute in the Soviet army during the Soviet-Afghan war. The word derives from *ded* ("dad" in this translation), which means "granddad" in Russian, and denotes a conscript who has been in the service for at least one year and by virtue of his seniority is allowed to exercise tyrannical control over new recruits, subjecting them to brazen exploitation amounting to hard labour and all manner of moral humiliation.

Before the era of *glasnost*, few people dared openly criticize the goings-on in the military, but then stories started appearing in the media of unheard-of brutalities resulting in permanent psychological and physical injuries and frequent suicide among the victims. It appears that the commanding officers do little or nothing to stop these practices and even tacitly encourage them in the belief that they teach the soldiers how to be strong.

Even in the absence of war, the army, anywhere, is a cruel, unsafe, closed world, perhaps more so in Russia due to its outdated compulsory service and poor economic conditions. Since the early 1990s, thanks to the growing movement of the Soldiers' Mothers Committees around the country, the public has been made increasingly aware of the harsh realities of life inside the army with its violation of basic human rights.

As is obvious from the stories in this collection, *dedovshchina* has a damaging effect on soldiers' physical and mental health. Army service is particularly deleterious to the sensitive intellectuals, to the boys from good families. Since men are drafted in their formative years the army easily breaks them morally, and often physically too. Often they are not able or willing to continue their education and participate in constructive activities after their time in the army.

Men's post-army adaptation is a universal problem: many former soldiers are not sufficiently articulate while others prefer to keep silent about their experiences. All the more valuable are first-hand accounts from those who can write well.

Pokrovsky and Terekhov have attracted considerable attention from both the Russian public and the press not only because of their shocking revelations but also because of their literary merits. They relate traumatic personal experiences without losing sight of man's better nature. Both writers avoid direct utterances and unambiguous verdicts, preferring instead to paint a picture through a mosaic of scenes and dialogues that allows the reader to make his own judgment. Both writers are known for their rich language and ready wit, which shine through even in translation.

See also the stories about the army in the "War" section of the Glas collection WAR & PEACE.

ABOUT THE AUTHORS

ALEXANDER POKROVSKY, born in 1952, has written seventeen books based on his twenty years in the navy. These are mainly cycles of satirical stories, both funny and frightening, about the trials and trivialities of life on a nuclear submarine. Based on the author's own experiences as an officer in the navy, they convince you of the sorry state of these underwater barracks that sometimes turn into common graves. Pokrovsky's picture of life in the Russian navy is less harsh than its prototype: he intentionally avoids traumatizing the reader, yet for those unfamiliar with the navy his stories make your flesh creep.

Pokrovsky grew up in Baku on the Caspian Sea where he enrolled in the Caspian Navy School and upon graduation was sent to the Northern Fleet. There he served on atomic submarines and also started writing as a way of "relieving the boredom of night watches". By the time of his discharge from the navy he had some 500 unpublished but widely circulating stories to his name. Today he has more than a thousand.

A number of his stories have been published in other languages, including one cycle in English in *Strange Soviet Practices* (Glas 34). In Russia, his books are printed and reprinted in hundreds of thousands copies. Pokrovsky is particularly popular in St Petersburg – where more than a million people used to serve in the navy – and other cities on the sea.

ALEXANDER TEREKHOV was born in 1966 in the provincial town of Tula in Central Russia. After serving in the army he graduated from Moscow University's Department of Journalism. He soon won acclaim as a writer with his stories about his army experiences and about the early perestroika chaos he was witnessing.

For his early novel *Buddy* he was severely persecuted by the Army Command. This novel together with a cycle of army stories, *A Conscript's Memoirs*, established him as one of the most talented Russian authors of the 1990s.

His next novel, *A Winter Day Starting a New Life*, describes his life in a rat-infested student hostel, a hungry but happy life in the early perestroika years of great hopes.

Letters of a Russian Traveller is a cycle of stories about the social ills exposed by the years of glasnost.

Terekhov's novel *The Rat-Killer* is probably still the best portrait of perestroika in the provinces. It draws a clear parallel between rat and human communities: as the phantasmagoric post-communist reality develops into nightmare, the greed, cunning and malice of the humans comes increasingly to resemble the behaviour of large communities of destructive rodents, while the rats acquire increasingly human features.

Translations of Alexander Terekhov's works include *A Winter Day Starting a New Life*, published in French by Editions du Rocher. *The Rat-Killer*, published in German by C.H. Beck Verlag and then by DTV, is due out in English from Alma Books in 2008.

"Terekhov's language is packed with forceful imagery and the slang of modern Russian. If we wish to identify precedents for his work we might look to Saltykov-Shchedrin from the 19th century for his satire of provincial life, and Platonov in the early Soviet period for his range of imagery and individuality of language. Terekhov, however, is a young and vital writer drawing very much on his own resources and experiences, with a distinctive and individual intonation." – *The Moscow Times*

Any undertaking in the navy goes in four stages:
First – terror;
Then – error;
Third – punishing the innocent;
Fourth – rewarding the non-participants.

"What did you see in the navy?"
"The neck of the man in front of me."
"And what were you doing the whole time?"
"Side-stepping problems."

Alexander Pokrovsky
SEA STORIES
translated by Noah Birksted-Breen

THE CHEMIST

"Where is that moral imbecile?!"

Did you hear that? The first mate is looking for me. Any minute now he'll find me and start shouting:

"Why the hell did you poke your nose in there again with that amputated brain of yours?"

And now let me introduce myself: submariner of the navy of Her Majesty Russia, commander of the chemical service on the nuclear submarines, or, put more simply – the chemist.

For eleven years, the Northern Fleet has cradled me in its arms and I've crawled along and made it as far as a captain third rank.

"Look at him grown into third rank!!!" the first mate would periodically howl and shriek when he managed to switch on his second signalling system and produce a stream of something resembling speech. And if the first mate was raging and fuming – then I knew I had done something right. I'd certainly grown into my rank.

Clever people get as high as first rank captains, wise people as high as third rank captains, and only legendary people ever make it to senior lieutenant.

One must choose between being a captain of the first rank, wise or legendary.

"Whoever you are, let the sun fill you with joy!" the ancient Greeks taught me, and I have let the sun fill me with joy. Only the sun, as there were no other joys.

The chemical division in the navy is always located near the bogs and the storage boxes with emergency gas masks.

"You've alchemised the whole place out here!" my boss used to say, and I always expected him to hold his nose in disgust.

A chemist in the navy is not a professional trade, not an ethnic label, and not even a final diagnosis.

A chemist in the navy is really a nickname. "He responds to the nickname 'chemist'."

"KEM-MIST!" they shouted at me, and I would run over as fast as I could, flapping my skinny legs like a hen on a conveyor belt running towards food; and they didn't need to give me further commands "Come here" or "Get out of here". I accepted my nickname "chemist" for what it was: the lowest possible starting point.

"Bastard!" they said.

"I'm sorry!" I replied.

"Punish him," they said, and they punished me.

"With your chicken brain you know your officer's

duties just as much as a chicken does!" they shouted at the very edge of my aural cavities. I clapped my sides with my wings and shouted:

"Cock-a-doodle-doo!!!" and was immediately cut down to size.

This is a "cluster method" in mathematics; you pick up a "cluster" – then, wham, right in the mug! Straight in the mug!

In the navy, they tested me for my "guts" and "backbone", for "what it takes" and "what it doesn't take", for "hatchability" and "pluck", and I passed all the tests with good marks.

"Lean your bucket over here!!!"

(My head, probably.)

"I'll give you an injection good and proper! I'm going to flog you!"

Yes Sir, I've bent over.

"Stop manifesting your absence."

Yes Sir, I've stopped.

"And hold back from your questions!!!"

I'd already been holding back.

And what can you do, comrade captain third rank, submariner of the navy of Her Majesty Russia? I can do everything:

From toast-master to street-cleaner,

From digging to flying,

From a gutter into the navy!

I can: carry, drive, shovel, pour, serve!

I can wipe things with damp rags!

I can do it all again!

But defend the motherland?

That's what "defending the motherland" consists of. The motherland starts with a floor cloth… for the submariner of the navy of Her Majesty Russia… including the chemist, excuse my foul language…

OXYGEN

"Chemist! What's your function d'you think in the navy? A meat-loaf?"

Our nuclear submarine is on a training mission. This is the fourth day at sea. The commander had called me over to the central post and now we're chatting.

"Where's the air, chemist?"

"Tssk, comrade commander," I spread my arms in the air, "a hundred and forty people came on board. I checked the entries. But the installation is only good for… (I quote some boring facts and figures), and the directive says… (figures, figures, and finally) … and it can't do more than that. You see, comrade commander."

"Why are you stuffing all this arithmetic down my throat?! I'm asking about the air. I'm suffocating. The oxygen everywhere is at 19%. Have you gone off your head? It's been only four days, we've only just kicked off from the base and you've already got no oxygen. So what'll happen next? If you don't have oxygen, bring it down in a bag! What are we meant to do: hold our noses, tighten our arses and stop breathing until you get us more oxygen?!"

"Tssk… comrade commander… I did warn you this submarine can only take one hundred and twenty people…"

"That's your problem! Go! Get out! If in half an hour you haven't got twenty and a half percent oxygen in all the compartments, I'll turn your insides out! I said get out! Stop munching your snot!"

Slipping down the ladder, I unburdened my soul and let off steam:

"A bloody ignoramus! A cavern! A terracotta chasm! That old corrugated… goat! Who's running this navy? High-school drop-outs! Kings of the parquet floor! Gangs of lost illusions! It's a shelter for the mentally castrated! A cemetery for rotten burgers! Mor-ons!"

Walking into my post, I screamed at the warrant officer:

"Idiots! Your name is legion! Walking waste of space! Make some air for him! The sort of idiots they draft into the navy! I'm going to stand like a generator now, with my hole pointing up, and I'm going to give him some air!"

I took a few deep breaths, calmed down and said to the warrant officer:

"Fine, right, anyway, go to the cabins. Move up the indicator on the gasometers. You don't need to add a lot. Make it up to twenty and a half."

"Comrade commander," I reported in half an hour. "There's now oxygen at twenty and a half everywhere."

"You see!" said the commander cheerfully. "It's become much easier to breathe, right away. I feel every degree with my skin. Chemist! Until I stretch your hide onto the globe… you won't budge."

"Yes, Sir. Permission to leave," I said, turned and walked off.

As I was leaving I thought: "He's feeling better. Ha! Pterodactyl!"

"HAVE HIM SHOT!"

The morning finally crept through the window and woke up the trapped flies, fate was ticking off the days from its yellowed list, and the commandant of the town of N., a moss-covered mayor, felt strangely sad, perhaps the same as a salad might feel when it begins to wilt.

His hair, eyes, lips and cheeks, neck and ears, arms and legs, everything pointed to the fact that it was high time either to hang himself or to demobilize. But demobilization, though inevitable, like the collapse of capitalism, didn't take a single step towards him and the days dragged on like the corridors of the guardhouse, and dripped and dripped onto the crown of his much-battered head.

The commandant had become a rotund creature long ago, but he still dreamed and all his dreams, as I already said, grasped pitifully at the sparkling hem of her Excellency Madame Demobilisation.

The door – there'd been someone knocking at it, obviously – opened just at that moment when all the commandant's dreams were still on the hem, and the commandant, coming to his senses and looking around at his assistant, the young lieutenant, who was standing right here, sighed and braced himself for the predictable surprises.

"Permission requested," a worn-out senior lieutenant appeared in the door and, having shifted from one foot to the other, he dragged in a soldier by the scruff of his neck. "You see, comrade major, he drinks! Every day he drinks! And another thing, comrade major…"

The voice of the senior lieutenant would have lulled the commandant to sleep, had he carried on for more than five minutes.

"So you drink? Huh, hero-warrior?" The commandant, with enduring melancholy, stared at the warrior's forehead where some signs of secondary education should be, he reckoned.

"Rotten deal," thought the commandant about the fact that he still hadn't been demobilized, and – with a groan – grabbed the chewed-up telephone receiver: the ear and mouth "saucers" on the telephone were so washed-out that it looked as if the commandant had wooden ears.

"Moscow? Ministry of Defence? … I'll wait…"

The commandant's assistant – a young, freshly-minted lieutenant – felt a creeping fear, like someone who sits on a bench after lunch, hoping to belch, and thinks about politics when a lunatic sits down next to him on the edge of the bench.

"Ministry of Defence? Comrade Marshal of the Armed Forces, Major Nosetickin reporting… Yes, comrade Marshal, yes! He drinks!... Yes… Every day… Permission requested…. We'll do that… We can have him shot… We'll inform his residence… Permission requested to start straight away… We'll do that…"

The commandant put down the receiver.

"Assistant! Where is our journal of executions?... Ah, there it is… So… surname, name, patronymic, year and date of birth… home address… nationality… Now, where's the executions schedule?"

The commandant produced some charts, then reached into the safe and pulled out a pistol, cocked it and put it down.

The assistant, eyes jumping out of their sockets, his lower half shuddering, his upper half hypnotically staring at the commandant's nape, at his very brain, was filling drop by drop with horror. Each new drop scorched him.

"So… the planned undertaking – the execution… the participants… now, the place – the parade ground, the obvious instrument – a Makarov pistol, sixteen rounds… the supervisor – me… executioner… My assistant! Listen, lieutenant, today it's your turn. Get used to our daily battles! You'll shoot this guy. I've already okayed it. Sign here. Please see it through. When you've whacked him…"

The commandant didn't manage to finish: both bodies shuddered and collapsed, the impressionable lieutenant – just like that, and the soldier – with a smell.

The commandant spent a long time tipping out the water from the decanter with flies onto the men.

He was moved into the reserves a month later. The commandant strode into the guardhouse for the last time and declared that, if he'd known it could be so easy, he would have started shooting people ten years ago. Flocks of them.

WHERE WERE YOU?

"Where were you?"

"Who? Me?"

"Yes… yes, you! Where were you?"

"Where was I?"

ComDiv-One – commander of the first division – is questioning Kolya Mitrofanov, the group commander.

"I was at my post."

"You weren't at your post. Where were you?"

The ship had just arrived from a practice outing for nuclear warfare and dear Kolya had jumped off the vessel in his quilted jacket and marked boots.

"Where were you?"

"Who? Me?"

"No, I mean just look at this vagabond... yes, yes, I mean you, where were you?"

"Where was I?"

It took Kolya three hours to hitch-hike his way to Murmansk. The pale lad was lucky. He was at the airport one hour after that. He got on a plane and flew off to St Petersburg. At exactly seven in the morning, he was in there.

"Where were you?"

"Who? Me?"

"Yes, yes! You, you, sonny, you – my precious, where were you?"

"I was where everyone else was."

"And where was everyone else?"

Kolya's overcoat was hanging in his cabin; with his boots and military cap. They noticed he was missing after about four hours. Everyone said he was somewhere around the place or maybe sleeping somewhere.

"Where were you?!!"

"Who? Me?"

"YES! YES! YOU! You bastard, where were you?!"

"Well, really, Vladimir Semyonovich, I mean really, where could I have been?"

"That's what I'm asking, where were you?!"

During the ten hours in St Petersburg, Kolya managed (a) to meet an unknown girl (b) to do a whole load of interesting things with her and (c) to fly back to Murmansk. He was absent, all in all, for twenty hours.

"I'm asking you again, where were you?!"

"WHO? ME?"

"Yes, you bastard, you! You… go stick a clarinet up your arse! Where were you?"

"I was in my cabin."

The ComDiv all but choked.

"In your cabin?! In your cabin?! Where were you?!!!"

I left the compartment so as not to hear this wailing of the Viennese woods.

THE BUTTERFLY

Officers never go off their rockers. They simply *must* not go off their rockers. They ought not to, in principle.

But it's true there are occasional instances of it. I remember a particular officer who was serving on the "Grozny", the destroyer. As well as three other posts, he also held the post of the mate.

They didn't let him on dry land for a year. At first, he begged, like a dog at the door: he kept applying and almost whining, but then he fell silent in the corner and went mad.

He was taken off the ship, put in a military hospital, later he was taken somewhere else, and then transferred to the reserves.

People say that when he was being taken off the ship, he was laughing happily like a child. That does happen here, of course, but more often than not, the officer starts pretending to be mad in front of the surrounding personnel, he behaves like an idiot because he wants to be transferred to the reserves – the officer, that is, – so he plays the fool.

Before, it wasn't so easy to be transferred to the reserves; before, you either had to drink like there was no tomorrow or, as I already said, play the fool.

But you could only play the fool when you had some talent for acting, when you had the appropriate physiognomy, when you had an inclination for improvisation, for playacting, or maybe even pantomime…

We once had a daredevil onboard. When toy butterflies on wheels went on sale in the local children's shops, he bought one for himself.

The butterfly was manoeuvred around with an attached stick: you'd have to walk around, pushing the butterfly in front of you, holding on to its stick; this also made the butterfly wave its wings.

He took it to his post, everyday, to work and then back home again. This went on for a long time: the butterfly happily ran alongside him.

The moment he began taking the butterfly around with him, he also changed: he was quiet all the time and smiled.

People tried to talk to him, to chat, to trick him into talking. They dragged him from doctor to doctor. And he went everywhere with his butterfly: the door would open and the butterfly would squeak its way to the doctor first, he himself was in tow.

And he went to the division commander with the butterfly, and to his commanding officer.

Doctors shrugged their shoulders and said that he was healthy… although…

"Now, then, look this way… no… everything seems to be… touch your nose."

The doctors shrugged their shoulders and declared him fit. Soon, he was transferred to the reserves. His pension would see him out. The deputy head of the political section personally took him to his train in consideration of his serious condition. The deputy even helped him carry some of his luggage.

The faithful butterfly ran alongside, fluttering around strangers' legs and veering around suitcases. It flapped its wings for the last time in front of the train: he climbed into the carriage but left his inseparable friend on the platform. The deputy saw it and broke out in a sweat.

"Vadim Sergeich!" shouted the deputy, grabbing the butterfly – after all, what if something were to happen in the carriage without the butterfly, he might throw himself out of the moving train to get it – the deputy would never be acquitted. "Vadim Sergeich!" the deputy was choking. "The butterfly… you forgot your butterfly…" The deputy was panicking, trying to find the door to the carriage.

"No need," he heard a voice from above, raised his head and saw him, calm, in the window. "No need", he said, looking down with wonderfully clear eyes, "keep it for yourself, my dear sir. I rolled it everywhere with me, now it's your turn…" And, on that note, he left, and the deputy was left alone.

Or, rather, he wasn't alone, he was with *it*: with the butterfly…

THE CURE

How can the nail on the first mate's toe suddenly cure the whole crew? I'll tell you how.

From an extended period on the strict "iron hulk", the first mate's fat, yellow right toe (the colour of a nicotine stain) began digging into his foot. This legendary event was accompanied by sniggering in the toilets and recommendations to wash his feet more often and cut his toenails. The officers' mess made snide comments:

"Grigory Gavrilovich is so busy with the threat of nuclear attacks that he's had no time to cut his toenails."

"And he's got no-one to do it for him."

"The statutes say that the commander must inspect his subordinates' feet on a daily basis – before night time for his whole personnel."

"The commander has totally neglected his first mate. He isn't supervising his feet. And when a commander abandons his favourite crew member, then that crew member begins to rot."

And so it went on. The longer it went on, the louder it got. It didn't stop at sly smiles. The first mate felt it with his skin — they're laughing their heads off at him, the bastards. He hobbled around for two more days and then gave himself over to the medics.

The doctors in the navy do things the easy way: they just amputated his nail, simply tore it off. As the foot was left alone, they then tied it to a slipper and let the first mate back out into the wild — off you go!

But only the commander, not the doctors, can release us from our work duties in the navy. The commander didn't release the first mate.

"Who're you expecting to take charge of the ship?" he asked him.

The first mate was actually expecting the commander to take charge of the ship, which is why his face darkened: there was nothing for him to do but to stay on board. He was ill in his cabin. From then on, nobody ever received permission for release from the first mate.

"What?" he'd say, when the ship's doctor asked for his permission to release this person or that from duty. "What?! He needs rest? At home? Have I understood you correctly? It's extraordinary! A high temperature? And I suppose you think his wife is an aspirin? You amaze me, doctor! He can be ill here. Tell him that's what I said. He can be ill onboard the ship. We have all we need here — sanatorium with a dispensary, God dammit. And I'll dispense it to him for sure. I'll scrub his gullet, if I have to. What? He has a high fever? So what, doctor? So what?! Are you a doctor or a prick in a coat? Go and cure him. Why are you rushing about, demonstrating your stupidity? Bring your thermometer here. I'll take his temperature myself. No fucking way! An officer doesn't just croak like that. I said, he won't die! What don't you get? Put him in your surgery, next to yourself. And sit there so he doesn't run away. And give him tablets. I'll be checking. And anyway, why have we got ill people? That's a minus on your work record. Where's your preventive action in the early stages? Huh? I need him back to normal in three days. On his feet, is that clear? I'm giving you three days, doctor. To get him on his feet again. Even if he needs crutches. Even if you're supporting him yourself. I forbid you from going on-shore until he's cured. So there! Bring your pass to me, it's going in my safe. On the double. People are your responsibility. Get used to it. People. What moral right do you have to leave the ship if your people are not in order? That's all! Go! And get everyone well!"

So there! From that time on, nobody on the ship was ill. Everyone was healthy, God dammit! And if any one of the officers or warrant officers made so much as a groan, then his boss would tell him immediately, imitating the voice of the first mate:

"Ill? Amazing! Stick this thermometer in your mouth, you turd. You can complain to Kofi Annan if you like. God dammit, don't be a wimp!"

And the sailors were cured with digging ditches. Occupational therapy. Basically, a profession-da-fé.

So there!

God dammit!

I AM ZVEREV!

If you've been floating around the navy for ages, you know everybody else. Like dogs from the same area, they run over and sniff between each other's legs: "he's one of us"!

If I don't need to tell you why there aren't any ill people in the navy, only the living and the dead, well then... you must know Misha Zverev, senior deputy head of staff in the nuclear-powered division of the navy, a captain second rank. When he received his "cap-two", he staggered along the wharf drunk as a skunk, still shouting at three in the morning, lit by the rose sunset, addressing the lower layers of the atmosphere:

"The Star! Found! Its! Hero!"

He had a young wife. Coming in from the sea, he always called her to announce:

"Kick them all out! I'm on the move!" And his wife met him, with everything ready, or as we like to say, "standing to attention", clutching at the hem of her skirt. And he never found evidence that he was a cuckold. Everything was always in perfect order.

Misha was always getting into scrapes and funny situations. Once he got a beating with sticks on the Riga seafront because someone ran off with a motorbike down the road (and let's face it, Misha's mug doesn't inspire trust.) Or he'd land in some other such mess.

He loved telling these stories to his friends. He would smile, looking dreamily into the distance and then recount them unhurriedly, with pauses for laughter and waiting for the slow-pokes to catch up. Usually, he'd start after lunch when everyone was already picking at their nearly-empty plates. The tale would begin with an oh-so romantic glance above their heads, at which point the assembled company would quieten down and, sighing, Misha would begin with a sad smile:

"I was born in Central Russia… at one of the railway junctures… I mean, fuck it … well, anyway… I was on leave so one day I decided to go to the banya[1] …"

In order to limit the quantity of "fucks" to the smallest requisite level, I'm going to tell you the story myself.

Before the banya episode, he'd grown a week's stubble up to his very eyes, put a quilted jacket over his naked body, a cap, denim pants, our navy sandals with holes exposing his toes; he put a venik[2] under his arm and set off, without hurrying in the slightest.

And it's mid-summer time: the birds are chirping; fresh air, flowers, he's in a good mood, free-do-om!

[1] A Russian sauna.
[2] A bunch of leaves from a birch tree, used to lash oneself in the banya.

It was noticed a long time ago that the further you are from the navy, the better your mood, and as you get nearer to the navy, your mood gets fouler and fouler, and when you're on board one of the navy's ships – then it's simply rotten.

Far from the navy, you breathe freely, you joke, you laugh merrily, you talk, you get up to any number of silly things, like the rest of the civilian population.

You need to pass by a railway juncture to get to the banya. As it happened, a special military train had stopped there. A guard stood by the first carriage. Well now, which honest drill officer would quietly pass by a private without saying a goddamn thing? It would be almost impossible, I mean just like a dog couldn't miss a lamppost.

Misha couldn't walk past. Overcome with solidarity, he stopped and then went over.

"Where are you coming from?"

The guard glanced sideways at him and growled, gloomily:

"We've come from… wherever we need to have come from."

"And where are you going?"

"We're going… wherever we need to go."

"And what are you carrying?"

"We're carrying… things which need carrying…"

"Fine, then, sonny, carry on serving and guarding. The motherland has entrusted you, so keep up the good work! I'm off."

"Where are you off to, uncle," the guard dropped his rifle from his shoulder and cocked the barrel, "don't move or I'll shoot…"

The captain, head of the special train, lifted his head from the table with difficulty. His face was blue-ish ("ich bin ill").

In front of him stood Misha Zverev, a pair of happy eyes looked out at the captain through his thick stubble.

"Hello, ha ha…"

"Hello…"

"See, they've taken me… ha ha…" Misha chortled inappropriately.

"He was interested," the guard came forward, "in where we're going, in what we're carrying."

"Well done, Petrov!" the captain managed through his coughing. "Have you got any identification?"

"What do you mean, identification, my dear boy?" said Misha. "I was going to the banya…"

"Well, well, well… We're not carrying a special department with us. So we'll hand you over at the main station."

"Comrade captain, I'm captain of the second rank, Zverev, senior deputy head of staff, I can bring you identification if necessary!"

"It's not necessary," said the captain, whose glance had stuck in Misha's stubble. "Sidorov!"

Sidorov appeared. He was three heads taller than anything you could possibly imagine.

"Right, Sidorov, lock up comrade... h-hm... senior deputy head of staff... that one there, the furthest staff carriage. Don't let him out to piss, he can do everything in there. Well, and so forth..."

Sidorov picked up the comrade (this senior deputy head of staff) under his arm and carried him to the far carriage, threw him in a heap on the floor and – with the words: "Gotcha, Misha" – he locked the door.

Misha just had time to think: "Horses have travelled in this train," when the train set off. As he was jolted forward, he quickly scuttled along on all fours, stopped, picked up his venik and laughed.

"Well, there you are," he said, "off we go... One carriage is as good as another." The echoing of clanging wheels disposes a person to reflection and so Misha settled down, onto the straw, to reflect.

They soon stopped. They'd reached a station. Zverev jumped up and was flustered. They would be coming for him any minute now. "Which station is this?" he kept on wondering and worrying. "I can't see a thing. God only knows! Where are they?" Nobody was coming to get him.

"Hey!" He tried to poke his head out of the window criss-crossed with barbed wire. "Tell the commander of the special train. I'm Zverev! I'm the senior deputy head of staff!" he addressed everyone he saw, but he just frightened everyone, one after another, with his unexpected physiognomy. One old woman was so deeply moved, from the suddenness of it, that she just said, "Oh my gawd!" –

weakened and collapsed on something that gave a slurping sound.

Misha burst out laughing and he laughed at her like mad until the carriage began to move again. They'd clearly forgot about him. The stations flashed by, and at each one he looked out for passers-by to shout at: "I'm Zverev! Tell them! I'm Zverev!"

Three days later, in Yaroslavl, they remembered about him ("Don't we have that... what's his name... that head of something guy?") and handed him over to the KGB.

In three days, he had turned into a wild, hairy, dishevelled creature, with wide eyes and a sharp Adam's apple. He smelt so bad that flies buzzed around him, flustered.

"Well?" the KGB asked him.

"I'm Zverev!" he declared with the face of your average convict. "I'm the senior deputy head of staff!" he added, not without some pride, and winked. He didn't mean to wink, it just happened. His mug could have been from any galley.

"Have you got identification?"

"Wh-at identi-fic-ation?" Misha choked for the umpteenth time. I was going to the banya! Look!" And by way of proof, he stuck his venik under their noses – the same venik he'd previously used to sweep the carriage.

"And what other evidence do you have?"

"What?"

"Well, to prove that you're Zverev."

Misha looked around himself and couldn't find anything. But then he remembered. Yes, he remembered alright! He had an uncle in Yaroslavl! Oo-oo! A dear uncle! They hadn't seen each other for twenty years!

"I have an uncle!" he exclaimed. "Oo-oo! Dear uncle! We haven't seen each other for twenty years! My dear uncle! Fuck…!"

It was already night when they set off to fetch his uncle.

"Are you so-and-so?"

"I'm … so-and-so…"

"Get dressed!"

And his uncle recalled a certain heroic epoch when you had to explain who you were in the middle of the night.

They brought his dear uncle over complete with his sandals. When he came into the room, a strange creature rushed towards him from out of a corner, with its tenacious arms thrown open.

"Uncle! Dear uncle!" it squealed unpleasantly, breathing through a rotting gullet, and scraping him with its prickly cheek.

"I'm not your uncle! Criminal!" The uncle broke free, slapping the creature on its hands.

Uncle was calmed down, and with the aid of the table lamp, he finally recognised his nephew and shed tears.

"It's just the nature of our job," they said to him, by

way of apology, "God only knows, I mean, what if suddenly…"

"Yes! Yes!" repeated the overjoyed uncle. "God only knows!" And he shook the KGBs' hands, then his nephew's hands, even his own hands. They drove him home – he was overjoyed the whole way back.

 "And you, comrade Zverev, if you want to, you can go straight to the train station. It's not far to walk. We'll let them know you're coming."

He got to the station at four in the morning. It was grey and damp and the ticket office was shut. Misha knocked and some old lady opened up.

"I'm Zverev!" He poked his mug through the elevated ticket window. "I need a ticket. They called you earlier."

"Give me the money."

"What money? I've got no money whatsoever! What's the problem, lady?" He started scratching the counter with his stubbly chin, "don't you have the slightest ability to understand people?"

The "lady" shut the window of the ticket office.

His nerves, shaken up by the carriage, the KGB and his uncle, didn't withstand this.

"I'm Zverev!" He began to thrash at the window. "I've come from the KGB! They called you! From the KGB! From the K! G! B!" he declaimed.

The ticket lady picked up the phone:

"There's trouble 'ere!"

Misha kept thrashing, over and over.

"I'm Zverev! Open up! Hey!"

The policeman had already been standing behind him for five minutes. He waited until Misha grew tired, then he politely tapped him on the shoulder. Misha turned around.

"Are you Zverev?"

"Y-yes…" Misha was very moved because someone at last had recognised him. He burst out crying and let himself be handcuffed. In the car, he fell onto the policeman's shoulder and, snotting on him, confirmed that he was Zverev, he was going to the banya, he had been at the KGB…

"We know, we know," said the wise policemen.

"And I'm also the senior deputy head of staff!" Misha stopped during one sob, shifted away and stared, hungrily searching for any objections.

"We see that, we see that," the policemen replied. The wise policemen handed him over to less wise policemen, and the latter locked him up till Monday. Misha started thrashing again.

"I'm Zverev! I'm Zverev! Tell the KGB!"

"And why not the UN? Kofi Annan, he might also find it fascinating," said the less wise policemen and shrugged their shoulders. "Look, it's just not on! You're not letting us work. Shall we knock him around a bit, or what? Just a bit…" And they knocked him around…

In the end, on Monday, everyone became clear about everything! (I mean, fuck!) The KGB and the police took

SEA STORIES | 39

him to the station, bought him a ticket, put him on the train and he set off home.

When he got off the train, even the geese staggered to get away from him. Misha made his way home through the back-gardens. As he got nearer, he heard music. There was a celebration going on in his house. Misha squatted down in the bushes. Life had taught him to be careful.

Soon, his childhood friend Vasya tumbled out onto the porch. He tumbled out, stood up with a groan and set off into the bushes, mumbling to himself and undoing his belt on the way. He stopped by the bushes, swayed, grabbed himself somewhere in the middle and, just then, a long thin fountain shot out of him.

When his fountain had squirted most of its reserves, a strange creation suddenly arose from the bushes, in his direction.

"What's going on here? …Huh? Vasya?" asked the creation, which had Misha's voice.

"I should have got utterly, completely legless!" said Vasya. "To have a vision like that…" and sticking his not-entirely-finished fountain into his trousers, he turned back to the house.

"Stop!" Misha overtook him with one step and Vasya curled up into a ball, as he was being dragged off.

It turned out that Misha's whole village had been looking for him with boat-hooks in the lake for ten days, and then decided: "that's enough!" and organized a funeral repast for him.

KUMZHA

"Kumzha" is a training course for generals at the academy of the General Headquarters in which they learn about submarines. A boat of every design is lined up for them, in the designated naval base. The boats shine with freshly painted insides, at the end of a week's industrial-scale tidy-up.

It's quiet, the rats are gone and the officers are waiting each in his section, in clean underwear and new slippers, all with new haircuts, and the PBDs are hanging in the right places, while the rest of the crew are led off to the navy club to watch films.

A crowd of generals, chatting among themselves, appears at the shaft-like opening of the hatch. The first of them begins to lower himself inside. Instead of turning his face to the railing, he's descending with his backside to it. So he's crawling down while his elbows poke into things on the way and this general gets stuck with his arms turned out.

"Hey, Vaska!" the generals standing above him are having fun. "It's not a tank, for fuck's sake, you need to use your brains here!" The ladder in the central area gently slopes down and people are meant to go down "face forward". Shifting back and forth before the ladder, the general Vaska turns (he's already "learnt from previous experience") and climbs down it with his back turned to the ladder, making a general's stride at each step.

"Vaska!" the generals shout at him again; they've just been explained, after "Vaska", how to go down the ladder. "It's not a tank, for fuck's sake, use your brain!"

The generals are given a guide but, once they're inside the boat, they still manage to get lost and crawl all over the place.

"Excuse me… where is the exit?"

"Down the ladder and then straight on."

"Thank you," says the general, doing everything he's just been told but ending up in a dead-end, which is a deserted storage hold.

"Hey!" emanates from there. "Comrades!"

In the first section, generals walk past the torpedoist's cabin. The last general lingers and hungrily looks at the PBD in this cabin.

"What an interesting flask."

"It's a PBD – a portable breathing device, used for complete isolation of your breathing organs in the event of a fire from the harmful influence of the outside atmosphere!" rattles the officer.

"A-ah…" says the general. "Look at that…" And he sees the officer's sandals: they have holes that make a sort of pattern: "Did you make the holes yourself?"

The torpedoist doesn't understand at first, but then he cottons on:

"The holes?… oh, that's… no, they were issued like that."

In the next group of passing generals, each general

looks with curiosity at the "flask" – all the generals have the same thought. The last one lags and asks:

"Is that a flask?"

Quickly:

"It's a portable breathing device!" This is spoken very quickly and almost hysterically, so the general only half catches it, but he nods understandingly, "A-ah…", a glance at the sandals:

"Did you make the holes yourself?"

Jokily and racing:

"That's how they were issued!"

Before the next group, the torpedoist manages to wink at the officer in charge of the next section: "What idiots, eh?!" The third group comes in and the last general in the group turns to the torpedoist:

"What an interesting flask."

The torpedoist is overcome with a fit of laughter. But, mouth trembling and bubbling, eyelids flickering, he tries to contain himself; his eyes are bulging, strange sounds pour out of him, this is, no doubt, a case of nerves. The general is surprised and he looks closely at the torpedoist. The latter:

"It-it i-is a b-bre-eath-i-ing d-d-d-de-vice!"

"Watch it," the general looks at the officer attentively, dangers bells are ringing, but here his glance accidentally falls onto the sandals, the general is animated again:

"Did you make the holes yourself?"

A ti-tita-an-ic effort is made to bring his face under

control (or he'd get it in the neck so he wouldn't be able to turn it), tears in his eyes:

"Th-th-at's h-ho-ho-how they issue them!"

The general, with sympathy:

"You've got the hiccups?"

A quick nod, trying not to collapse.

Not everyone gets as far as the missile section, only the most curious. The commander of the section, captain of the third rank Sova (fifteen years in this position), buttoned up to the larynx (he has no neck from old age), explains to the general that he has sixteen ballistic missiles under his supervision.

The general with respect:

"I imagine the minister knows about you?" (The general has only three missiles in his base, but there are sixteen here.)

"No, no!" says Sova. "Even the flag-officer can't tell me from other officers."

Soon, Sova is fed up with the generals, they've tired him out, and suddenly he bends in half when the next general comes in.

"What's the matter with you?" the general jumps to one side.

"Cramps… fuck it… comrade general."

"Careful!" fusses the general. "Have a seat!"

Everything comes naturally to Sova: the tears, the wheezing… he grows into his role, he groans and twists his face until they lead him out and carefully sit him down, leaving him alone. When there's nobody beside him anymore, Sova sighs meekly, undoes his collar in one jerk and, leaning against the wall, he rolls his eyes and says with feeling: "What a load of wankers," after which he falls asleep in a split second.

At the same time in the central section one of the generals from the infantry sees a contraption called "Chestnut". He says with a cavalier accent:

"What's this?"

The first mate, his uniform pressed, with a tag on the breast pocket, all rigid from tension:

"This is the 'Chestnut' – our military transmission device."

"Oh really? Interesting, and how does it work?"

"So, you see," the first mate, like a magician, clicks a switch, "Eight!"

"This is eight!" croaks out of the "Chestnut".

"There you have it," says the first mate, bringing the "Chestnut" back to the starting point, "you can talk to any section."

"Yes? Interesting," the general lingers by the "Chestnut". "May I?"

"Certainly."

The general turns it on and unexpectedly speaks timidly with his old man's thin, trembling voice:

"Ei-gh-t... ei-gh-t..."

"This is eight."

"Can I talk to you?"

Silence. Then the voice of the eighth section commander:

"Well, talk… old chap… if you've got fuck all else to do…"

"What's happening?" mutters the general. Struck dumb, he clumsily turns his head and looks around with wide eyes.

The first mate is confused and dreams of giving a good bashing to the eight; but suppressing this wish for now, he mumbles:

"You understand, comrade general… military transmission… commanding words… in a word, he didn't understand you. You need to do it like this," the first mate sharply leans to the "Chestnut", bares his teeth on the way as if he is ready to bite, and roars:

"Ai-ght!!! Ai-ght!!!"

"This is eight!"

"Get closer to the "Chestnut", eight!"

"Yes, Sir, I'm closer to the "Chestnut". This is eight!"

"That's how you do it, comrade general!"

The generals leave. It's time for lunch, the sections relax and there's laughter; the officers have come together in the fourth for a meeting, everyone already knows – they're teasing the commander of the eighth: "He says to him: let me talk to you, and this guy says well, talk, old chap… the first mate almost keeled over and lost his guts. Get ready for anything, there'll be a bucketful of blood, he'll turn your balls inside out."

"Well, well... I'll just keep saying: "Yes, Sir, I'm an idiot, Sir!"

TRAINING

The frost blew... Those who have experienced this kind of frost know you *can* put it like this. The weak sun, size of a kopek coin, was muted by the grey sky. Under the grey sky sat a saboteur. He sat on a hill. He had an impermeable coverall, with fur inside, electrically heated and hooded. He also wore boots. High ones. Home-made Russian boots, waterproof. And the saboteur was also home-made but a hired one, from the saboteurs' unit. He spent the night there. In our snow. And now, he was eating. Vacantly. From our can. He twisted-turned-opened something in it and began to eat at once because the can had a self-heating device.

With the broad and measured movements of his horse-like jaws the saboteur was simultaneously watching the foothills. He was waiting for them to come and get him.

The third day of training went by. Implacably. Our boys were learning to repel an attack on our naval base by this type of electro-fish-horse.

A defence headquarters had been set up. An operational unit had been put together, which would catch these hired horses with the help of a combined platoon of Eastern wolfhounds.

Information update: our Eastern wolfhounds are small, sinewy, tough, courageous. And handsome. In their own way. One and a quarter metres tall. But the main thing is: they don't think. If they get hold of something, they don't let go. And the other main thing is: there are lots and lots of them. Take as many as you want because there are more where they came from, as many as you need.

The wolfhounds arrived from different places with their overcoats and belts, their boots stuffed with flannel foot-bindings; they fed them in the waterfront galleys with ordinary army food, the type of food you can only eat with ideological conviction, and set them onto the saboteurs. The one thing they forgot was to hand out mittens. But that's a minor thing. And, in any case, soldiers from Wolfhound-land are different: their hands only freeze in the first six months. And if you have anything to say about the food, we'll answer you this: if you can feed the army well, then why have an army at all!

Then came the third day of training. On the first day, the other side, dressed in all of our things, captured the headquarters. This is how they did it: they divided into two groups, then one half took the other into captivity and led them straight into the headquarters. And the sub-lieutenant saw through the window that someone had taken someone else and shouted:

"Soldiers! Who did you get?!"

"We caught some saboteurs!"

"Good lads! You'll all be commended! Bring them straight to me!"

And so, they brought them. Straight to him. And thus they occupied the headquarters.

On the second day of training, from the side of the polar night and the shiny waters "the fish" sailed over and "mined" all of our boats. The last "fish" came on shore, dressed in the uniform of a first-rank captain, more specifically of an "inspector", according to his documents; he arrived at the checkpoint and gave a workout to the guard at the top...no, no, no, just the observation over the waterfront. Because he didn't look in the right direction. Watch the waterfront and nothing else. The whole time! As if you're glued to it! Unblinkingly. Do what you're told. Without fail. See there? Right.

And the guard watched as he was told while "the first-rank captain, the inspector" dropped by, on his rounds, to the division commander, whose headquarters were located next door. (On his way there he asked the guards: "Are you keeping watch?" They replied, "Yes, Sir." – "Well-well," he said, "keep it up!" and he walked on.) Then he arrested the division commander, dragged him out of the window, went down through the opposite section and took him away in an inflatable rubber dinghy. Actually, they say that the division commander himself inflated the dinghy under close supervision by the "inspector". But they're probably lying. The boat was already inflated by the oarsmen and was moored by the special storm-ladder, which had been lowered into place. It was made of silk. Very comfortable. And it was a good boat too. A dream boat.

Naturally, the captain of the watch saw that a boat was moving in another sector but he was responsible only for his own sector and therefore didn't report it. That is how the second day ended.

On the third day, the task was to capture the saboteur alive, the one on the hill. There he sat and waited for this to happen. And our lot stood at the foot of the hill, pointing up at him and conferring agitatedly. There were twenty of them and they attacked with resolve, led by their commander. Even he had joined the attack.

"Circle the hill! Kasimbekov! Go in!" the commander finally gave the order and they began to circle and go in.

The wolfhounds dug through the snow, wading out chest-high into it, they swam in it and circled around their target, unstoppably. At their head was Kasimbekov. Less than forty minutes had passed when the first of them had swum up to the saboteur. This first one smiled joyfully and tried to catch his breath.

"Stop!" he exclaimed. "Hands up!" After which, all of his strength left him, and only his smile remained. The saboteur finished eating, stood up and kicked the first man. During the next fifteen minutes, the rest of the attackers congregated at the same place where the first one had stood. The following ten minutes were dedicated to a "physical conversation" between the wolfhounds and the saboteur. The former never ceased smiling and, in the eastern custom, were shouting ecstatically, flying through the air with their white foot-bindings, and then crumpling the bushes and flying-flying-falling back down with their foot-bindings wound around their necks. It was great! Then the saboteur gave himself up. He said: "I surrender."

And they took him, alive. They packed him up and carried him in their arms.

That is how the third day ended. We began to win from that day on.

THE SPEECH

The speech was a long time in the making. It was decided that each person would have to give a speech because our ships were going to pay a friendly visit to the French city of Marseille. Everyone was ordered to write a speech in advance, and that's what they did. Then everyone was called up you know where and they read to them their speeches and explained what they had written and that these were not speeches but the raving nonsense of a legless mare and dog crap. Everyone was ordered to re-write their drivel and so they all immersed themselves in magazines and newspapers; and they duly re-wrote their speeches. Again, their efforts were considered and they were told: "Comrades! This is just no good at all!" At which point, they were made to sit down at one big table and someone dictated what they were supposed to say. Next, they were instructed *how* and *when* they should give their speeches. They were told to keep quiet unless they were asked to speak. Then, to each speech an element of individuality was added in case they were asked to give them at the same time. Finally, they checked them all again, they streamlined them a bit more, sharpened them in a few places and screwed them tight. Everybody was told to learn his speech by heart. "You'll be tested", they warned. A deadline was set. And everybody was tested. They were told to be more accurate. A new deadline was set. Again, they were tested and it was certified that everything was as it should be. Finally, the speeches were stuffed in everybody's mouths, into their pockets I mean, and we set off for Marseille.

In Marseille, it turned out that our lot were the dear guests of the mayor of the city of Marseille, and so everyone was taken to the town hall. The table was laid, there, full of all the right things: bottles, bottles, bottles and finger-foods.

The mayor of the city of Marseille took the floor. He said that he was immeasurably pleased to welcome these envoys of a great people on French soil. A drink was offered after that. Everybody drank.

Two hours went by. Drinks flowed non-stop because one Frenchman after the other stood up to explain that he was unbelievably pleased. Then, all the Frenchmen, as if following orders, collapsed onto the table and fell asleep. The mayor of Marseille was asleep at the head of the table. Only our guys were left. They carried right on: they gathered in groups, raised their glasses, chatted and argued…

At the end of the table sat one greying captain second rank, a mechanic. Red and sweaty, he was drinking alone, not arguing with anyone. He looked straight ahead and only lifted his glass to his lips. Somehow, without noticing it himself, he reached into his inside pocket and fished out a bit of paper. It was his speech. The mechanic was surprised. He looked at it thoughtfully for some time, without comprehending.

"… The time…" he began reading in a preacher's voice, at which everyone around the table fell silent, "when our two na-ations…"

The mechanic's eyes bulged wide; he didn't understand a thing he was saying but he kept reading:

"Our two… well anyway… they're coming… they're coming… hic!"

He began to hiccup, although he managed to bravely suppress the hiccups:

"They're coming… lads… hic!… to a historic time…. hh – ii – cc!…"

His hiccups became longer and deeper, and our guys were smiling more broadly:

"At this time… hic… we all want… hic… you see, we want, you know…" The hiccups came in quick succession now, and the smiles around the table turned into laughter, then from laughter into raucous belly-laughs.

The mechanic stopped, smiled, washed down his hiccups with wine from a tall glass and, looking at the paper, said dreamily: "Fuck it, eh?"

THE INSPECTORS

We have more admirals in the navy than we know what to do with. And there's one particular breed of them, which is specially trained for inspecting. It's in their blood.

They check everything. Once a week we're visited by a bastard, I mean a commission. Of course, the navy's used to them – just like animals at the zoo get used to the public gawping at them. Now only the top brass gets anxious, but even for us the inspectors are a bother.

"But," you ask, "why can't they send reserve captains to do the inspections?"

Apparently, they can't. We've got a load of reserve captains of our own, so if they sent someone of the same rank, we'd pack them off to read the graffiti in the gangways. And that's why admirals pop up all the time.

All admiral-inspectors have slightly skewed brains because of their non-stop inspections. Their brains are on a kind of slant, with a kind of a twist. However, you can never guess the angle of the slant, so to speak, because it's different each time.

Of course, if the inspector's been coming every day, you plan ahead and predict individual episodes or occurrences, but to foresee the whole visit, so you can sleep soundly at night... well, that just ain't going to happen.

There's one, for example, who loves stopping his car, calling over an officer and, without so much as bothering to get his body out of the car, starts testing whether the officer knows article 82 and 83 of the disciplinary code. So... spit it out! What's written in articles 82 and 83 of the disciplinary code?

It's interesting and instructive to watch a serviceman passing such a test... but to watch an officer is far better. People are going about their business while the officer is sweating it out, it's as if he is trying to squeeze a blackhead out of his forehead with the sheer weight of his desire to get the right answer. And there's a kind of warped expression which takes over the officer's face. "82 and 83?" "Yes." But he's stuck. His mind's gone blank. He can't tell you for the life of him. He mumbles that he knew it a moment ago, earlier on, he was... but it's slipped out of his head. Just vanished. And he was even reading those articles a short while ago. Those very articles, as it happens − 82 and 83.

Sweat is pouring down his face; he's a trembling wreck. Of course, the officer is more than happy to sweat; and his heart only beats on command and stops on command. If he's a real officer, that is.

So the admiral is watching him squirm from his car,

waiting. This admiral's got only one living emotion – love of salmon – because the rest were all suffocated in embryo.

Another inspector, in his sunset years, no sooner arrives than he asks to see the scrap heap. He gets to the scrap heap and says:

"But you've got a goldmine here!" Meaning you can bring everything back and add it to the inventory?

We all listened to him, naturally, with much trepidation, but nobody could work out what exactly he meant. What was the gold in our scrap heap? He took that secret to the grave.

There was another admiral, too, just as old, a real old goat, his head was sagging but he was still serving, the poor dear. He loved the word "shit-house". "You've got a real shit-house here," he'd say. A shit-house was as much as he ever managed to see when he was inspecting the navy.

Then there was an admiral who just loved bolts. He gave a yearly inspection. They'd made a bolt out of stainless steel, and nickel-plated it too, specially for him. It was placed vertically on a stand and capped with top-notch glass.

But each year, the bolt had to be made a few millimetres thicker and taller. There were blueprints of this monstrosity lying around somewhere in the navy's factory. Their handicraftsmen chiselled these souvenirs and our top officers presented them, slobbering all over their sleeves.

He would give the previous bolt to the officers in his company. He used to call up a colleague and ask:

"Hey, listen, have you got a bolt? No, not that type of bolt. A souvenir bolt. You can put it on your desk." And he gave them all away.

Everyone in his division had been "bolted" by him.

But the most original admiral of all, the admiral with the biggest screw loose in his head, was the one who inspected us at college. He was kind of short, kind of grey and kind of fat; he had whitish eyelashes. His nickname was "The pig'll find the dirt".

He'd arrive in the company followed by a watchful crowd of subordinates. The man on duty – his senses dulled by responsibility – would rush up to him, half-bent over: "Comrade admiral..." to give his report. He'd listen to the report, turn to the subordinate and whisper: "The pig'll find the dirt". Then, he'd set off to the toilets.

Of course, everyone knew that's where he'd go, and they were ready for him but they'd always forget something or other: he'd crawl all over the place and – invariably – he'd find something wrong. Well, you just can't keep up with him!

One day, he set off decisively for the toilets with his subordinates hurrying behind him in a frenzy, but he went straight into a cubicle. They shot after him but he closed the door. There was a silence. They were all standing there, looking at the door, waiting.

Suddenly, from under the door came a hoarse "pull!".

Nobody understood what to do but they all stuck their heads up like turkeys, ready for anything. Again, a hoarse: "go on, pull!" So, the bravest of the lot stepped forward and tugged the door of the cubicle: the latch came off, the door opened and… there he was on the bog, oops, the admiral, oops, with no trousers on, sorry. Everyone craned forward. And the admiral said: "So, can you see?" – and they all leaned in, as if their lives depended on it: "What, where?" – they all shuffled as close as they could get, and anyone who couldn't get near the cubicle stretched up on their tiptoes, levered themselves right up to get a glance.

They looked as hard as they could but they couldn't see anything other than the trouser-less admiral. Well and his bottom was as wrinkled as an accordion in the process of shitting. So, then what?

"Just like that!" said the admiral. "A person's sitting in here when someone else yanks the door open. The latches are old and the door opens – it's enough to make anyone lose his appetite to do his business. Where's your compassion for your fellow man?"

And then everyone looked at the problem again, this time from the other side of the door, really thinking the problem through, and then set off noisily.

And the admiral stood up, happy, pulling up his trousers and then doing them up – with whatever happened to be in them.

After that, we replaced the latches with bolts so you were only able to pull them off with superhuman strength.

A PRESENT

The First Vice-Admiral of the Navy went down to the central post of the nuclear missile-carrier.

The commander came to meet him, walking slowly with shaking, jelly legs.

The Vice-Admiral heard his report and said:

"I won't go further than the third section. Guard, is there water in the hold?"

"No, Sir!"

"First mate, is there water in the hold?"

"No, Sir!"

"Deputy commander of the political department?"

The deputy commander swallowed hard and shook his head:

"No, Sir!"

"Commander! Also, 'No Sir'?"

"Yes Sir, 'No Sir'!"

"Well, let's go and have a look." There was plenty of water in the hold.

"Lantern!" barked the Vice-Admiral.

The lantern wouldn't light. The first mate grabbed the emergency light but its handle fell off.

"Well, well, well…" said the Vice-Admiral… While he was walking along the jetty, they were looking for the key – the key to the life-saving safe. That's where the "traditional present" was kept – a little boat made of ebony. In a panic, the key had been stuffed somewhere out of the way.

"Where's the key!!!" the commander dashed back and forth in the central post.

"The key!!!" he bellowed so loudly that it echoed all around.

"Break it open… break it… break it…" muttered the deputy commander of the political department, through deathly-pale lips, as if in delirium.

In the end, they found the key. The commander himself got down on all fours to open the safe. The key wouldn't fit in the keyhole for a long time. The commander raced to catch up with the Vice-Admiral.

"Comrade… admiral… of the navy… here's… this is for you… from us… a present… tradi… tional…" he breathed heavily, almost suffocating.

"I'm going to rip you to shreds, and you're sticking presents under my nose? Fi-ne! I'll check you on your return from sea…"

For two weeks the boat stayed at sea. It moved up and down the same square – this way then that way - until the Vice-Admiral of the Navy had left.

THE BUOY

The monstrous sun blazed impudently; large dewdrops grew into fat, glinting puddles on the rocket-carrier's deck; the repulsive blueness of the dreamy skyline dropped a sinful longing into our souls to be finally let out on leave, and our inflamed imaginations were picturing horrific scenes.

Our dear sub, that submerged "heap of iron" packed with the latest engineering spasms of Russian genius, the natural beauty around and the brevity of our cruise, along with the miraculous organisation of the navy, did not lead to a substantial alleviation of the desire to get on all fours and bite someone.

The morning coldness woke us, like a bastard, and the air – soiled with negative ions – seemed as slippery as a jar of canned meat.

Some plane flew over us, greedily embraced by the sun, and threw down a few pieces of rubbish. The sub made a turn so we could lasso the thing and drag it onto the deck.

"Signaller and the head of radio-engineering on deck!" said the captain. The team rushed below and soon enough, the signaller, and behind him the head of radio-engineering, nervously climbed up on deck. They both declared that the lassoed object was a radio-buoy.

"Is it American?" asked the captain.

"Yes, Sir!" they replied, and people gathered around, curious onlookers with cutting tools who were burning with the desire to take the enemy to pieces.

The captain nodded, and the curious onlookers started making a racket, as they surrounded the foreign present. But, just then, they heard a ticking. It went very quiet.

"What's that?" asked the captain.

"Comrade captain, it's better not to open it," said the head of radio-engineering, "it's probably a self-detonator."

The curious onlookers found that their desire to duff up the enemy was shrinking to miniscule proportions.

"We could sod the whole thing and get going?"

"Comrade captain, if we don't open it, we could easily carry it around for a year."

"Really?"

"Yes."

"Fine, we'll take it to the base and deal with it there."

"Comrade captain," the signaller remembered suddenly, "they have a microphone in it which transmits everything to the USA."

"Really?"

"Yes."

"Then everyone below deck!"

Only the captain held his ground on deck. He waited until everyone had disappeared, and then bent down to where he reckoned the microphone must be.

"Can you hear me, you stinking American bastard: burst your fucking locators! You'll see how red, peeling stumps will hang from your bodies from the might of Soviet power!" And such feverish turns of phrases poured forth that even the most patient bit of wood would warp under its weight, most people's ears would twist into a shell while they themselves collapsed altogether.

The captain got so carried away, swearing non-stop, that he knelt down in a daze, using his hands to demonstrate, sticking his fingers into his mouth, champing them and tastily licking them all over. His face shone with ecstasy the whole time, with a sort of radiant passion. He was, in a word, alive, pulsating, existing to the full.

When they brought the buoy to the base, it turned out that it was one of ours.

THE MEDAL OF THE BALD FUCK

We called the Vice-Admiral Artamonov, our divisional commander, Artemus or, more often, "General Kesha". And all because when checking the fulfilment of the military task by the crew, he behaved like a true general: in other words, like a lout, in other words, he poked his nose everywhere.

He loved giving orders and taking charge of the ship, as well as interfering in everyone's business, whether they were navigators, radio operators, hydro-acoustic technicians, helmsmen or holdsmen.

What's more, he had so much energy that he managed to ruin things for everyone, all at the same time.

And what do our beloved Naval Statutes say on this particular topic? They say: "Don't stick your nose into other people's business."

But nobody's tongue would stir to remind the admiral tactfully about this rule, that is, tell him in so many words: "Where do you think you're going?"

Once, we went out to sea on an assignment with our "General Kesha" onboard, and he gave us a real nightmare. When Kesha started picking on the boatswain for the umpteenth time, the vertical steering jammed and our nuclear submarine – phased by all this nonsense – which had just surfaced at that time began to chart out concentric circles in the water to the great surprise of the fishing seiners, scattering in all directions to dodge us, and the reconnaissance schooner "Marianna" which was observing all this madness.

Then Kesha barked something to the holdsmen, making them immediately re-set the mile-counter to a zero.

And, when every living being had witnessed the collapse of the mile-counter, our navigator appeared on the main deck – one estimable Alexander Alexandrovich Kudinov, the greatest specialist who was known for his obstinacy. Alexander Alexandrovich has the nickname "Long time ago". D'you remember that Hussar song: "Long time ago, lo-ong… time… ago"? Well, our Alexander Alexandrovich – or Al Alich for short – was "long time ago" in three ways: he became captain third rank a long time ago, he became bald a long time ago, and – a long time ago – he became chief of the military navigation deck. Another similarity with the hussars: when he was beside himself with anger, he would grab at anything nearby and throw it at anyone who made him mad, but since his subordinates never bothered him, and his superiors did, he threw himself exclusively at his superiors.

He was such a hurricane that his superiors couldn't immediately comprehend what had hit them, and they only comprehended it several days later when Al Alich was already far away at sea.

On this occasion, he couldn't find anything to throw but he did find something to say:

"What the … (and after this, he said exactly twenty seven words most of which rhymed with "muck". Which words did he choose? Well, for example, truck, duck, luck…).

"What the …", Al Alich repeated himself, "fuck, who re-set my mile-counter?!"

Everyone on the central deck had a "Masha swallowed the ball" expression, and then everyone on the central deck remembered there was something they hadn't yet done, according to their schedule. General Kesha became purple, jumped up and began shouting:

"Navigator! Have you gone off your head? How could you? Just you wait…"

Unable to express the feelings, which had welled in his angry chest, the divisional commander flew into the navigator's cabin, carrying along the navigator with him. The door of the navigator's cabin slammed shut, and all sorts of sounds were then heard from within: a shriek, a squeal, the stamping of feet, a crocodile's howl and the noise of smashing plates.

While precious crystal was being smashed and human beings devoured alive in the navigator's cabin, everyone on the central deck were sensitively listening to the breakdown of who-what-when-why-how. All this time, the boat was sailing off wherever it wanted.

Finally, the door of the navigator's cabin flew open. The divisional commander darted out with eyes bulging like a wild owl's. While he flew into the commander's post, a thin backcombing of his hair tumbled off his head – it had been painstakingly fashioned as a flat strand of metre-long hair across the bald spot from the one place on the divisional commander's head: behind his left-ear. The backcombing collapsed and the divisional commander's hair flew after him, fluttering in the air like the tail of a wild mare.

The divisional commander rushed to throw himself into his chair, squeaking with humiliation. His hair, calming down now, hung from his left ear to the floor.

The navigator poked his head out of the door and shouted after him:

"Bald Fuck!"

To which the divisional commander reacted just as tersely:

"Bald yourself!"

Kesha-the-general was upset by this incident for a long time. But it has to be said that, despite his looking like a loutish peasant, he was not stripped of a certain dignity. When Kudinov was presented with a medal and his papers turned up on the divisional commander's desk, at first he fussed about, made a face, pretending not to remember who exactly this Kudinov was, then he seemed to remember:

"Yes, yes… a decent specialist… decent…" and, slowly penning with his intricate flourish, he signed.

But the navigator didn't receive the medal in the end. That medal never even reached the navy – it was nicked somewhere above ground. So our navigator ended up without a medal. But anyway sometime later, instead of a medal, by way of consolation, the divisional commander removed an earlier reprimand for "loutish behaviour towards a senior", and the whole story was called: "the reward of the Medal of the Bald Fuck".

THROUGH THE PERSIAN GULF

All's quiet. "Ivan Kozhemyakin", the submarine mother ship is crawling through the Persian Gulf. The commander's on the bridge. The commander's favourite expressions are: "leave my balls alone" and "stop pricking around"! The night's pitch-black. In the darkness, on the ship's starboard, some sort of coast guard boat is barely discernible. It is accompanying our mother ship so we "don't go where we're not wanted."

"A flare!" barks the commander. "Otherwise, we'll squash it in the dark by mistake, then we'd need to apologise in English and I only studied English for half an hour, at school, if you add it all up."

The commander and English: yes, he'd be mentally constipated, whereas in Russian, it's the other way round – pulsating, seething streams. In the Suez Canal, our mother ship was at the head, which is why we were entitled to a pilot. When this dark brother came on board, he greeted the commander:

"Mornink, captin!"

"Hm…" the commander replied.

"How doo yoo doo?"

"Hm…mm…"

And it was forty degrees in the shade. Our lot were packed onto the bridge: first mate, second mate and other riff-raff. All wearing ties, service caps and shorts – the tropical uniform. Heads melting under these puffballs. The commander made everyone dress up like this: what if they suddenly ask us "How doo you doo?"

"Doo you speek Inglish?"

"Nao."

"Oh, captine!"

The commander turned to our lot and said through clenched teeth:

"Have I asked you, monkey-man, why you don't speak Russian?!"

Things were better at night. Cooler.

"One more flare," said the commander, "they're not responding for some reason."

The mother ship is old, like a container for leftover food. One day the diesel engines stopped working – for three days, we quietly sailed off somewhere into the distance. As a general rule, there's always something breaking down.

The little guard boat still doesn't reply.

"Well, okay," said the commander, "let's blind them with our floodlights!"

Some time passed as we worked out who's going to do the blinding and how to blind them.

Finally, we worked out how to do it. The envoy switched on the wrong thing and whatever he switched on almost killed someone or other. Then we switched it on, properly, but again it was no good.

"Comrade commander, the phase's blown!"

"God, you whores, you boiled cunts, get all the electricians here quick!"

The electricians were all standing on the bridge already. The commander calmed down – after pouring some more filth on them – and grandly targeted the guard boat.

"Well, now, blind them!"

The floodlights were turned on but they were too weak, dammit, and didn't even reach the boat. The commander looked at the mechanic and screamed four of our favourite letters.

"On the galley, comrade commander, I think there's a good little lamp," the mechanic illuminates him, "on the galley!"

"Right, bring it over."

They made a racket, running up to the galley, unscrewed the lamp, made a racket running back, screwed it in, switched it on – it was only slightly better.

And suddenly – a column of fire in our eyes, like the sun, nothing visible, painful. Everyone's hands shot up to cover their eyes. What was going on?

The light rushed over to the side, everyone took their hands from their faces. Ah, so that's it: the guard boat had lit us up with their super-powered floodlight.

"Comrade commander," someone asked after a silence, "shall we hit them too with our floodlight?"

"Hit them?" the commander comes back to life, "No, no. That's enough. And I, like an old fool, said: light up our brother from the Arab Emirates. Ha! If only one bastard had said: forget it, comrade commander, don't even hope to get them. But, no! But I still said: light him up! Yeah! If he lights us again with his floodlight, we'll all drown! What floodlights are you talking about! You are all dismissed, great nation!"

It's getting dark. The commander's alone on the bridge. He's suffering.

OH, THOSE RUSSIANS!

Our commander was given the task of photographing the American frigate on duty, so he was given a camera with a metre-long lens tube, and taught how to use it.

The commander called over the head of the RTS and taught him how to use it, so that he shouldn't forget himself.

The head of RTS called over the sergeant-major of the crew and, to be sure that something should stick, he began to train him.

The sergeant-major of the crew called over a sailor and gave him a lesson in photography, to shore up his own newly learnt skills.

In a word, everything was ready: the people, the ship, the camera. And the frigate was somewhere nearby.

At some point during the day we surfaced... To the Mediterranean... In a sultry heat... The sun baking our necks... Circles in our eyes...

Then, suddenly, the American frigate – for God's sake, here it is, the sonofabitch – takes it upon itself to make an approach. The commander yelled from the bridge: "Bring the camera up! Quick!"

The frigate was approaching amazingly quickly. We dragged the camera up.

"Now, we'll get a picture of it alright," said the commander and pressed himself to the camera. It was visible, of course, from where he was but it would be better from higher up.

"How's the RDP, first mate?"

"All in order, as always, comrade commander."

"I know your 'all in order'. Bring it up. I'll sit on the platform and you can hoist me up slowly. And tell your...

these sons of the rising sun of yours that if they drop me, I'll tear their heads off."

RDP is our sliding telescopic device. It extends our range of possibilities, which are anyway colossal. It's a large pipe. And on top of it, there's a float large enough for a man to be hoisted on it.

The Mediterranean has never seen anything like it: our naked, stick-thin commander, with a scooped-out stomach and a metre-long lens around his neck, slowly floating upwards.

"That's enough," shouted the commander and the ascension stopped.

The frigate was already right beside us, and so the commander pressed to the camera again.

"Now, down!" shouted the commander after a couple of minutes.

Something happened below. Something got stuck.

"It's been lubricated, it was working yesterday," the first mate all but wailed.

The frigate had hurtled off long ago and our half-naked commander was still sticking up high above the sea's calm surface, waving his camera and howling at the top of his voice.

Next day, the Italian newspapers printed some huge photos. They showed our sub with the raised RDP and the commander with his scooped-out stomach rushing around, from his neck hung that miracle of technology – a camera with a metre-long lens. Separately, they'd printed a close-up of the commander's wailing face. The caption underneath the picture read:

"Oh, those incomprehensible Russians!"

We didn't have any luck with our own photos – in the heat of the moment, we'd forgotten to remove the cover from the lens tube.

FOR MOTHER RUSSIA

Russian sailors are best left alone, it's best not to drive them up the wall. I know that for sure. And now I'd like to elaborate on this point with some specific examples. But first let me say: our Russian sailor needs little or no excuse to fight for his Mother Russia, for Holy Rus, for his faith, the Tsar and the Fatherland.

And even if he can't get his hands on anything, he'll tear you to pieces with any sticks at hand – with sticks, with stones, with teeth, with fangs, with hooves.

To digress a little from the main plotline, I'd like to recall how at one recent historic point in our navy's history, a strategic map of the Mediterranean was brought before the eyes of our historical Commander-in-Chief. It depicted a huge American aircraft carrier side by side with our tiny little cutter keeping track of the former.

"What's this, then?" exclaimed the Commander-in-Chief of the Armed Forces. "What is it? What?!" He kept poking and pointing at our tiny little ship but our staff officers just couldn't understand what he meant, they just didn't get it.

Finally, it dawned on them: our ship was drawn as just a tiny dot on the map.

So, they drew it again: they drew a small aircraft carrier and next to it a huge Russian patrol cutter; and then the Commander-in-Chief was pleased up to his bald spot.

So anyway, coming back to the main plotline, let me say this: "Yes, comrades! Yes! The airspace of our beloved Motherland is invaded by anyone who can be bothered. Yes!"

Of course, we do have a thing or two to bang at them, we can ruffle a few feathers except that we're tied up, hand and foot – tied up, belted up, welded together and bandaged over. And in spite of our confined circumstances, we're expected not only to shuffle around like penguins in a flock, but we're also obliged to stave off hostile attacks.

"Our Armed Forces are duty-bound…!" we hear from all over the shop – those who remember from all the shenanigans only what the Armed Forces owe them personally.

We know that we're duty-bound, who's going to argue with that? Well, obviously. But what would you say: can we ram them? No, we can't. They don't let us ram. They don't allow us. Now, if they let us ram, then we'd show them. We'd be ramming right and left.

Did you hear how we recently rammed Americans without permission? That was a day of triumph.

It was like this: in the Black Sea one of their cruisers – a displacement of thirty thousand – infringed on our territorial waters and immediately our SKR, as old as the moorings on the Neva, rushed to intercept it.

It was nothing less than a swan's song to see our ancient grandpa SKR patrol boat intercepting their modern, fat, self-satisfied giant. Plus, inside our grandpa, everything was panting, squeaking, shrieking and smelling foul. And yet everything was trembling in anticipation of a fight.

"Well, fuck me!" said the captain of the SKR, which had been ordered to go over but had been forbidden even to bark at the Americans; it was meant to go over and do something or other, but at the same time sod all, nothing which would violate anything international.

"Well, fuck me!" said the commander of the SKR. "I'm going to give him one!"

And he gave it to them – he ran into the cruiser head-on. He just went over without thinking and ran into it. The American shuddered. He wasn't expecting it. He was dumbfounded. But ours didn't cool off, it backed a little way off and then again – bang!

"HA-HA!" yelled the captain of the SKR in total ecstasy. "HA-HA! Don't you like it?! Got stars spinning around your head yet? Don't you like it?"

The SKR kept moving off and then throwing itself at them again, and the American just kept on putting up with it. It was the moment of our greatest triumph.

Finally, the American decided (before he got a hole drilled in his side) to slip out of our waters. He turned around and tore off with all his strength and our teeny SKR, completely maimed by the encounter, risking its remaining health, followed it into the neutral waters, trying to catch up and ram it in the bum.

Next time, the next American cruiser again intruded into our sacred borders in a totally different place.

So, who went to deal with it this time? That's right – a coastal patrol cutter. The cutter went up to the cruiser and said that if it didn't get the hell out of our waters immediately, then it – the cutter – would open fire.

The cutter even aimed at it with its farter, that even in still weather would not as much as dent a bullet-proof vest. And they stood alert.

"To hell with it, with my career," said the cutter's captain, pulling his cap on tighter, "I'll give them a symposium on disarmament right now, even if my soul perishes."

But his soul didn't have a chance to perish. The cruiser, having sent a message by transmission: "Impressed with the courage of the Russian commander!" turned and sailed the hell out of our waters.

Also, dear citizens, in the open sea, the planes of our likely enemies fly over our vessels, both submarines and surface ships, right over the upper decks; they fly around, the swine, wherever they want, they fly so skilfully that our teeth grind in helpless rage, and our hands reach for anything which could replace a machine-gun – nuts and bolts, for example.

Did you know that the deck of our ship is the holy of holies, our native land? And the air space above it right up to the ozone layer – I can't remember how many kilometres – that's our own air space. And the enemy's climbing into our airspace and hanging above our native land – hanging so close that he can bash us in the face.

And he is hanging there, as I've already said, not only above our surface ships but also above our submarines, which happen to be in surface positions.

Once, a foreign helicopter was hanging above our nuclear-powered submarine, it was hanging right above our missile launching deck, when a door in the helicopter opened, and some guy crawled out. This guy sat in the door, swung his legs over the side, grabbed his "Leika" camera and started photographing us.

"Give me the submachine gun," shouted the commander. "I'll *photograph* him now. He can feed the fish, the bastard."

They looked for the submachine gun for a long time, then its tripod, then the keys for the cartridge box, then they opened it and it turned out there were no cartridges there, then they found the cartridges, but they'd put the tripod somewhere.

The captain howled. Finally, someone ran over and brought him a can of condensed milk; and the captain hurled the can at the photographer.

The helicopter tore off to one side, the photographer all but fell out. He shouted at us as he was flying off with hearty Dutch swear words and shook his fist, but our lot laughed obscenely at him, pointing at the jar and shouting:

"Hey! Do you want some more?"

Well, we're allowed to throw things. Especially if they're trying to immortalise us on film so impudently.

There was one time our anti-submarine boat was sailing along a foreign shore and suddenly a vessel from their border guards peeled off from their shoreline and moved towards our boat. It levelled up and went alongside us. And immediately a man with a tripod appeared on its deck; he started setting up the tripod without fuss, without hurry; then a camera appeared with a metre-long lens and the photographer began to walk around the deck, as if in a play, measuring us up to get the full length.

As he was getting ready, our boat's cook climbed up on deck, a midshipman of depressing proportions, a certain Popov.

"Huh, you insect," said midshipman Popov, observing the enemy.

Then he went down into the galley, and he brought up a potato the size of a hockey-player's helmet.

"Hold on to your lenses," said the cook and, without aiming, he let fly his potato.

It was thirty or forty metres to the vessel. The potato flew as if from a cannon and blew up right on the photographer's head.

He fell nose-first onto the deck and lay there for a long-long time while the vessel ever so quickly turned round and rushed back to shore. It carried our victim back, snivelling, to his mummy.

Everyone was dying to know where the cook had learnt to throw like that.

"You should play gorodki... you know, skittles," said the cook. "Then you'd be able to hit a deer in the eye one kilometre away."

When I heard this story I thought: maybe we really should teach everyone in the navy to play gorodki – and have done with it. And we'll be hitting deer in the eye. Although we probably don't really need to hit deer in the eye. We only need to hit their heads so that their eyes pop out by themselves.

ABOUT SCIENCE

How does science come aboard the navy? Science tends to arrive aboard unexpectedly and always right before departure, as the boat is about to set off – and there it is. Some pale research assistant turns up with a box, comes over to the boat and asks the upper watch:

"Would you mind if my box stays here for a while?"

The watch shrugs and says:

"Put it over there..."

The research assistant puts his box beside the watch,

then he goes over to the "Chestnut", our sub's communication device, and requests our central post to "please kindly" come down to find someone he can hand this valuable box over to. The box contains a unique device (five of them in the whole of Russia) that is supposed to accompany our nuclear submarine on this voyage. While the research assistant goes down and looks for someone to give the unique box to, the watch changes and a new watch is already accepting the box as a given, something which belongs to the jetty. The first watch goes down and the first mate appears up above.

"What's this?" the first mate asks the new watch and kicks the box.

"This?" the watch looks at the box with the eyes of an orphan from Central Russia.

"Yes, yes, what's this?"

"This?..."

"This, this," the first mate begins to show impatience, "what is it?!"

"This?..." the watch asks thoughtfully and looks at the box studiously.

And now the first mate starts yelling, because the whole raw mass of crude experiences connected with the preparation race preceding the voyage, the whole heap of hot worries and anxieties, the whole weight of the last few days sitting heavy like a shaggy dog on the sagging shoulders of the first mate, suddenly – from these unhurried reflections of the watch – break, in one instant, that most fragile of things on earth: the delicate spine of a first mate's patience.

"Gr-r-r! I a-m a-s-k-i-n-g y-o-u, w-h-a-t t-h-i-s b-o-x i-s!" yells the first mate, all of his extremities shaking horribly.

The watch gets very scared, he loses his voice, his honour, his conscience, control of his face and he stands there like a gawping idiot. In his eyes is deathly horror. You wouldn't be able to beat a single word out of him now.

But the first mate is gushing unstoppably: he shouts that the Motherland has given birth to lots of idiots and all these idiots have filled his ship to the very brim; you could put a bomb under these idiots' noses or even amputate some bit of them (the idiots), but they wouldn't even budge; you could wrap them up in wet rags and kidnap these idiots with no problem if you want.

"You, pitch darkness!" howls the first mate. "Why haven't they already wrapped you up and kidnapped you?! Why hasn't anyone stolen this wonder?!"

Then, he kicks the box several times and, grabbing two sailors, he barks:

"Now, take this crap and chuck it so far that I'll never see it again!"

The sailors take it (the crap) and, in compliance with their briefing, they begin to shift it: they drag it onto the planks of the jetty and – one-two-three ("It's bloody heavy, this crap,") – swinging it back-and-forth they throw it into the sea.

And then just imagine that utter human sorrow, that inexpressible anguish which contorted the face of the research assistant who had finally climbed back up to get his box. The best of my poetic efforts wouldn't suffice to describe the super-human pain and tragedy on his face. I'll quote from the classics instead: "Symorgh, the bird of Grief, spread its wings over him."

ATOMIC ENGINEER IVANOV

An officer died – the submariner and atomic expert Ivanov. The devil take him, you might say. Why not just do a whip around and then forget about him, particularly as he didn't appear to have relatives or furniture of any value, and he'd parted ways with his wife a long time ago – his wife actually wished he would croak in the gutter. But he died, in the first place, without leaving a note along the lines of "I'm dead, blame such-and-such", and in the second place, he died on the eve of his fifteenth patrol mission. He would have lain there alone for god knows how long without anyone bothering about him but he was expected onboard that same day. So they waited for one day more and then reported him missing to the HQ.

That's how this whole thing started. There was someone knocking on his door at regular intervals while the rest of the crew spent their long weekend looking for him over every hill and in every basement. His friends were questioned whether he might have got held up with some woman. In other words, they looked everywhere for him but couldn't find him. Finally they put a permanent post outside his door and washed their hands of the whole thing. And it didn't occur to anyone that he was lying in his own apartment and that he'd long since given up the ghost.

Desertion was soon on everyone's lips, and the political department demanded a profile of him; the crew became agitated again. As panic took hold, his profile started to resemble a criminal's; it was noted that he had long ceased to be a good example of military and political acuity, that he showed a disdainful attitude towards political studies, and that he was so off-hand about current events, he hadn't even bothered to prepare a summary of them as he should have.

For a long time, they wondered whether to write that "he was basically politically-minded" and that he was "committed" to his work, or whether to leave that out, finally they decided it wasn't worth writing.

In his service record – to give him a rounded public persona – they added five disciplinary punishments and twenty disciplinary warnings; they urgently put together two "transcripts" from the officers' court of honour; then the first mate, noticing that there was still space in the document to mark him down, missed him out from any political-educational work.

All the collected documents were handed in to the personnel department and, immediately ordering some poor guy straight from the patrol to take his place, they left, hoping with all their hearts to land him in prison.

The personnel department, when they'd checked all the documents, ascertained that his last reference was positive in fact.

They re-wrote the reference. They re-wrote it in such a way as to make it perfectly clear that he could, in principle, be working as a submariner, when all's said and done, but that basically it would be better to put him into the reserves for discrediting the noble rank of officer.

Some time passed before it occurred to somebody to open his apartment. They opened it to discover the mortal remains of the atomic expert Ivanov – there he was, poor chap.

The flagship doctor's workload increased. He had to fill in a whole pile of papers not least because it was established that he had been in full health at the moment of death. The truth is it turned out to be harder to discharge a dead man than to find a living man.

They never found his medical records: they must have been on his sub that went to sea on patrol. In a panic, they rushed to compile it from his notes in the logbooks but as they hadn't managed to find all of these, everyone came to their senses and realized that they'd have to do without.

The flagship's doctor enlisted two young doctors to

take care of this affair, and, having done that, he gave a great sigh of relief.

With the help of our gallant police, they managed to find Ivanov's twice-removed aunt, Maria, who had lived, it turned out, in the very middle of our vast map, in the village of Small Makhalovka.

"I can't come right now though," the aunt responded with a quick telegram, "I live alone, I'm already an old woman, I have a cow, how can I leave it? And the potatoes are ready."

They picked a reliable officer, a captain-lieutenant, from the navy's discharged personnel and entrusted all the funereal duties to him.

We have plenty of officers like that in the reserves, discharges from the navy's active duty. They build out-houses, dachas, they dig pits and ditches, help with the potato harvest, look after haymaking, they organize clean-ups, lay down turf, fix front doors, shape up all sorts of things till the cows come home, and generally do a lot of useful things.

This particular officer had been discharged twice in fact. The first time it was on account of an ulcer – or was it a kidney stone? He'd filled in all the forms for discharge according to that particular article and he'd handed in the forms, and would come each day and wait in various queues. But then it turned out after a month that he'd handed in the forms god only knows where, and he'd given them to god only knows who, and that nobody – at the place where he'd handed them in – recognized him in the slightest.

"How could you be so careless?" he was told. Right there and then he had some sort of a stroke, some sort of a Latin disease struck him, or possibly Latin American, and after that he could be discharged according to a totally different article. All this to say, he was reliable.

The "reliable" one set off to the shipyard to get zinc. The coffin needed to be dressed in this zinc so it – along with the prematurely deceased Ivanov – could be called "Registered Cargo No. 200".

The shipyard knew about the zinc business but they still rebuffed him: the limit for zinc had already been reached and more zinc was due to be delivered later in the month.

"They called you to have it ready, didn't they," Reliable fought back weakly like the last Spartan.

"It's different times now," he was told.

"Now what am I going to do with the body?" Reliable wasn't calming down because, from childhood, he'd learnt never to give up.

"Well, where's he been kept till now?" the bulging-eyed shipyard tricksters asked him with their faded voices.

"At home," said Reliable, uncomprehending.

"So let him carry on lying there, it'll be fine, it's already cold. The only thing is you'll need to open the windows, of course," now shipyard people stepped over to advise on the second stage of corpse-maintenance: "and make sure you empty the water from the radiators and switch them off. We can help with that. What type of radiators have you got? DU-20s? So you see…"

"What do I 'see'?" The Discharged Reliable didn't see anything. "How can you help?"

"With all that," the factory workers were surprised by his grasp, "we'll switch off the radiators, we'll send a welder over."

"No, I'm afraid this isn't good enough at all," the 'Discharged' began to object.

"Well, we don't know then," at which point, they turned away from him and forgot he even existed.

With this "we don't know", the discharged officer decided to speak to his superiors right away. Along the way, he cut the air with his hand as he mumbled all sorts of curses.

"Huh! I wish they'd all drop dead!" he concluded.

This was the first time the captain had had a 'zinc problem', and after ten minutes of walking he decided definitively to go to his superiors, because he felt certain they had thicker skulls and heavier jawbones.

"And I thought he'd been buried a long time ago," his superior with the jaw looked up from his papers, having long forgotten about these worries and that someone had at some point died in his department. "Did you get the collected money for this? So! What were you thinking?"

"What have you done to get zinc? Why didn't you get any? Why didn't you insist?" his superior asked with increasing volume. "What's the point of standing here in your complete uselessness?"

"Go and get it!" his superior had eventually started yelling. "And stop demonstrating your hopelessness and total lack of ability! You must dig! Dig! You're not captain-lieutenant for nothing, are you? Dear God, what utter ineptitude! He can't find zinc! Open his mouth and put some in – he'd shut his mouth and swallow it! That's right, isn't it?! I! Am Not Here! To Get! Zinc!!! Do you understand? Not To Get Zinc! Get out. And don't cover your lack of work with petty fussing around! There must be zinc! Don't report back without it! Get out!!!"

Vitamins in the navy come in tin cans, but they ought to come in buckets or maybe even barrels…

The captain left his superior. On his way back, he kept saying three words, of which only one was very much like "… yourself".

He disappeared for nearly two days, then turned up crumpled, with a guilty appearance and took up the task again with fervour.

But in the meantime, the doctors had asked around, on the quiet, about zinc, and finding out when it would arrive, they said: "Fine, we'll wait," and immediately agreed on a wooden coffin.

"Wooden?" the shipyard latched on to this. "So you won't be needing a zinc one?"

"Yes, we will," said our unperturbed doctors, "both zinc and wooden. For now, he'll be lying in our morgue."

And so they put him down there. When the zinc finally appeared and they'd made what was required of it, they unsuccessfully tried to cram in the carefully preserved Ivanov – he didn't quite fit. He was twenty centimetres too big on all sides.

"Who measured him?" asked the manager of the shipyard when this discrepancy had infuriated everyone. It turned out that the measurements had been taken by a sailor who had already been sent into the reserves.

The manager of the shipyard unburdened his heart with some elaborate oaths and said: "Next time an officer must take the measurements!" He thought a moment and added, "Captain-lieutenant, squeeze him in! Now! Even if the whole crew has to push him in. You'll suffer here... for the Fatherland. I'll make you into a man..."

After this, the shipyard workers split their efforts: some fulminated at Ivanov for not fitting in as they kept on squeezing him into the box with gusto; the others tried to cajole the doctors – they followed them, looking into their eyes ingratiatingly. After a few minutes, they decided it was time for action, so they began:

"Well, maybe, we can chop off a chunk of him somewhere, eh? A small one, eh?" Their voices kept nagging at them, temptingly. "Nobody will notice, what do you reckon? Then, we'll bury him ourselves. Or maybe you have something that would do the trick? Maybe, we can pour something on him, to dissolve him a bit, eh? It's all the same for him now, what do you reckon?"

"We're not sure," said the doctors, shaking their heads and walking away, leaving Ivanov at the shipyard till the evening. He was due to be sent away in the evening. And they had train tickets already, no wonder everyone was in despair.

"Do what you will," said the manager of the shipyard to the head of the section. "Cut him or eat him, just make him fit! Make him fit! Even if you have to lie in it yourself and stretch the coffin! D'you want us to bury you instead of him? In short, it's your problem!"

The head of the section really wanted to get the job done; he had grown so weak with wanting that he was ready to lie in it himself to try to stretch the coffin. But suddenly everything worked out. In the navy, everything works out eventually, everything turns up trumps, sorts itself out, you just need to stop yourself getting stressed about it…

In the end, five determined and tough-looking lads, with a good quantity of colourful expressions, squeezed the atomic expert Ivanov into the wooden and the zinc coffins, like dough into a jar. They jumped on top of it and squished all of him in. They knocked in a few well-aimed nails in the places where bits were trying to squeeze out. No problem at all…

At that very time, back in our neck of the woods, they tried to find a car, the Discharged Captain rushed around, blind from grief. He'd already established that right now out of eighty two cars – of which thirty three were jeeps and the rest were out of order – only one was ready for active duty, a lorry of sorts: and to be more precise, a rubbish truck.

Sick from his bad luck, the captain was nevertheless ready to take Ivanov, now soldered into the zinc, in the rubbish truck.

"What are you thinking?" they said back in the rear and didn't give him the rubbish truck. He still managed to get Ivanov to the station, by hitchhiking, while generously watering his way with regular half-litre bottles of vodka. They got to the station with twenty minutes to spare before the train's departure.

"Where do you think you're going?!" bellowed the woman conductor and blocked his way.

"We have permission," the captain whispered, with a voice dulled by his journey: he had travelled the whole way on top – outdoors – in minus twenty.

"Get back!" the conductor didn't give way. "I'll give you 'permission'! Where would the people sit?!"

She shoved the captain and his box off the train. The captain, totally weak with hopelessness, took out the money collected for Ivanov's funeral and, utterly ashamed of himself, he offered the conductor a reward.

"Well, okay," she said, taking pity, "drag him back on, I'll show you where to put him."

They dragged the coffin where she was pointing. Just as the train started, the chief conductor turned up.

"Where are these burying-men?" The chief conductor

looked like he somehow already knew who'd shitted where and what was causing all the trouble.

"You, is it?" he jabbed the captain with his finger and the captain's pulse started racing. "Yes? Show me your papers."

The captain shouldn't have panicked. His shaking fingers finally managed to get the papers out.

"Well, I knew it," sighed the chief conductor, "it's the wrong one. Get off at the next station. Don't forget to grab your friend. I'll come and check. I know your type, we once had a scoundrel like you here. He gave us lots of problems."

Some more cash was produced… When all is said and done, good people still exist, they do; just now, he was bellowing at you, spraying you, but *now* he's a good man and you've started to love him, experiencing the deep joy of forgiveness.

"Next time you have to transport someone like this, make sure you fill in all the forms correctly," said the chief conductor, grabbing the captain by the shoulders. "Oh, and also, careful where you put him, sometimes cars on the trains are stripped bare, to say nothing of your relative. But zinc has value; you'll come back and it's been pinched – no more zinc and the dead man's been travelling naked. That happened once, I'll give you that one for free," the chief conductor chuckled.

The captain ran out of the train at each station to check. And the long journey began. Many things make a journey what it is. You're travelling past things and other people are travelling past you in the opposite direction, talking about meat and butter ("and how's it where you live?"), children, mothers-in-law, presents, vacations, holidays. What won't people talk about? What haven't they lived through? And you feel like you're from another planet, as if you haven't even lived yet…

Two days later, he felt like he'd been living on this train for ages, that he was born here, among crying children, among squashed up sleeping bodies, endless snacking, tea-drinking, and legs sticking off the ends of the bunk beds getting in everyone's way. He gave in to indifference and now he sat looking straight ahead out of the window, as if he were a lookout. And Russia rushed to meet him… Russia… this huge land…

The captain had to change trains. I won't describe it or I'd have to enlarge this story by a third. Let me just say out loud: "Good!" Good that people drink. Or maybe not people, just individual citizens, but it's still good. How many things wouldn't get done, like that, on the hoof, at one sitting, if drink wasn't involved. Our captain would never have made it on time with the zincified Ivanov from one station to the next. Let them drink. Because if they didn't drink, then you'd probably have to inoculate them to get things done – to replace their drinking habits. Probably, you'd have to…

But look, here's Small Makhalovka, identical to thousands of empty white stations up and down our country. Not five days had gone by.

Two people met the train – an auntie and a bearded man. The captain sensed with an inner nose which was auntie Maria and the end of his journey; he was filled with happiness and a desire to jump for joy.

"Here he is!" exclaimed the captain after some five minutes or so and, expending all the sweetness he had on a smile, he pointed to the coffin: "It's him!" He almost added: "Isn't he handsome!" but he stopped himself in time.

He felt good again. This 'goodness' spread over him wave after wave and now he was just pleased for himself, for Ivanov, for everything around him, for himself again, for auntie Maria, as if he'd brought her a lump of gold, not a coffin. And so it was, the further he was from the navy, the more pride he felt in himself; and pride in our navy's military preparedness, he felt strong bonds of kinship…

"What else… papers, photographs – here!"

"Listen, my dear," auntie Catastrophe said hesitantly, "but really … it's not actually Mishka … Ivanov… I remember him as a young boy, haven't seen him since … I can't quite remember but his hair was more blackish, and also he was sort of snub-nosed, but this guy's sort of bald, wouldn't you say?"

A child of the navy had momentarily stepped on shore. The captain broke into an uncontrollable sweat, everything around became damp and disgusting.

"What do you mean, auntie!" the earth began shaking under his feet, "HOW CAN IT NOT BE HIM?"

"AUNTIE!!!" he bellowed, pouring into this shout all his wounds, despair, zinc, the train conductor, the journey, God only knows what. "Auntie! It's... not a curly little boy, it's a ... a man, and also he's... it's ... under the sea, a submariner, auntie, a submariner, and you don't look like yourself down there, you wouldn't even look like a horse down there!"

"Well, fine, then... of course... don't be... I didn't think..." auntie Maria quickly agreed, very afraid, staring guiltily at her feet. Beardie understood right away what the problem was.

"A spitting image of Mishka," he was also afraid that maybe the funeral feast wouldn't take place, maybe this captain would grab the coffin and vanish with it into thin air, "a spitting image. I've known him, the bastard, known him since he was that small," (he measured out twenty centimetres). "A spitting image."

"You see!" The captain heaved a sigh of relief. A whole stack of good health, which had almost left him, returned. "Ye-e-ssss, well, auntie, you really... ! Not recognizing Mishka, eh? Ye-e-sss...!" Now he felt good again, somehow even looked younger too.

"Well, anyway, citizens," the captain waved his hand vaguely. "Now you're going your way and I'm off my way. I'm sorry if anything..."

"No, hang on, dear friend, what are you...?" Beardie was standing next to him. "Brought him and then he wants to rush off? So, 'you're off that way and we're off that way' and that's it? And the feast? And the people? We won't let you!" and he suddenly took the captain by the elbow. The man had a wooden hand and the captain understood – he really wouldn't let him go.

"But… the navy is also waiting… warships…" he mumbled in defence.

"It can wait, it won't collapse," Beardie cut him off, "our people are waiting for you. And anyway we'll make you a chit… print one off… saying you fell ill or something," Beardie began to bellow with laughter so that in front of him a little old lady with a bag sneaking past sat down in shock, turned her head and squeaked: "Police!" – and rushed off into the distance.

So it was – everything was ready. They dealt with Ivanov in a flash. Nobody could remember, in the end, whether he actually had black hair or was maybe bald from birth. The festive dinner table shone with autumn magnificence. Everything came in bucketfuls here: in the middle of the table stood such a giant bottle of homebrewed vodka, of such size and transparency, that a raised stool on the other side could be fully seen through it.

Old men and women, dressed in their Sunday best, gathered for the funeral repast. Decorations and medals shone on the old men, a whole glowing radiance. One century-old grandpa, with a silver beard to his waist, had four St. George's crosses from the time of the Tsars, besides various other medals.

Twenty minutes later, everyone at the table was the best of friends. The old men kept looking with interest at Mishka's medals – which he'd won for ten and fifteen years of irreproachable service. They kept passing them around and, one after the other, they turned them around and read the inscriptions aloud.

"Ye-es… We never got ones like these. This is what they're like nowadays. Good boy, Mishka, good boy, you didn't put us to shame, ye-es…"

Soon, the captain decided that he ought to say something – he imagined that in a couple of minutes he wouldn't be able to say anything, in a couple of minutes he'd only be able to mess the whole thing up. He stood up and began to talk, at first with unconnected phrases but then more and more fluently, about the navy, about the sea, about Mishka, whom he'd never known, but actually about himself and his own life, about the daily service, about the navy's brotherhood which – though it burns with a bright flame – will never burn out, about the Motherland, about all the men who are defending Her now and, if anything happened, would give their lives for Her, about the sacred national borders…

"I wish them all the best," the captain's voice rang out in the hushed silence, "I hope they don't burn, don't drown; I hope they always have enough air; I hope they always make it back from under the sea; I hope their children are waiting for them on-shore, their wives still love them, they deserve love, comrades, they must not go unloved!" So, you see, his words flowed smoothly and with style and maybe people listened to him properly for the first time in his life, maybe he said what he thought for the first time in his life; and tears shone in people's eyes, maybe this was all happening for the first time in his life… Suddenly, he got a lump in his throat and he stumbled, waving his hand; everyone jerked forward and some old woman who, like all the others, not quite getting what he was talking about but seeing that the man was suffering, pressed her hands to her cheeks and muttered:

"Oh, Lord, you poor thing, poor thing…"

The repast was going full steam ahead. Everyone wanted to exchange kisses with the captain. One ancient grandpa, in particular, was having a bad time getting to the captain:

"Grishka!" he belted out. "Damn you, you swine, are you trying to get in a second time? Go on, shoo!"

Huge Grishka, who was over sixty, got embarrassed and let the old man past.

"Well, now, my dear chap… let me give you a kiss!"

Then they sang sea songs: "The glorious sea – the holy lake Baikal", and then the captain taught them all a new song "The northern navy won't let you down"…

Soon, they carried him outside, put his cap on him and seated him on a bench. He sat there and cried. Tears trickled down his face, still unshaven from the journey, collected on his chin and dripped into the greedy sand. He muttered and threatened emptily into the darkness –

he'd probably imagined or remembered something from his past, which only he knew about.

The grief subsided and now he was laughing hoarsely, he shook his thin head and slapped his knee; then he repeated about twenty times: "To die in the navy – not on your life!" upon which he fell off his bench, smiled and fell asleep.

They picked him up and carried him into the house so he shouldn't fall ill. They let the captain go home a week later. He slipped auntie Maria the rest of the money, even adding a bit from himself. Auntie felt bad, waved her hands, said that she wouldn't take it, that God would punish her for taking it.

They remembered him for a long time afterwards, wished him all the health God could grant him, happiness in his personal life and many children.

And soon afterwards, someone in a huge, black overcoat burst into auntie Maria's house, grabbed her and hugged her mightily.

Auntie stopped breathing as she recognised Mishka, her snub-nosed, black-haired nephew, just like he was as a child...

She weakly pushed him away, sat down on the fortunately positioned stool behind her and froze.

She didn't hear how Mishka was yelling. Her face had somehow grown more pointed, she felt how her heart was beating for the first time – hanging on by the tiniest of threads. Her lips opened, she sighed: "God has punished me," fell softly from her stool onto the floor and died.

They said in the village that "her time had come" but the autopsy showed that she had been completely healthy at the moment of death.

There was a funeral repast. Mishka, who was told that they all believed him to be dead, got drunk and sat in the corner, singing. The others were singing "The glorious sea – the holy lake Baikal" and "The northern navy won't let you down".

SUNDAY

Today's Sunday. But how's it different to other days of the week? It's not like you can get off the ship because it's Sunday. Everyone finds a corner to sit in, and a film's playing in the crew quarters, but tomorrow's Monday and everything will begin to drag on again for the whole Week. That's how it is, lieutenant Petrukhin. There's a knock at the door.

"Yes."

A messenger comes in.

"Comrade lieutenant, the first mate is calling you."

On the way over he thinks: what for? He felt sick at heart.

He couldn't recall any errors. Then again, who knows. He's been on the ship for a year and the first mate has done nothing but tear him mercilessly to shreds and always for some rubbish, and always watching him like a boa watches a rabbit. Maybe he's been in the crew quarters again and found something or other there?

"May I?"

The first mate was sitting at his desk but, despite the colossal glare, the lieutenant understood that he wouldn't be torn to shreds this time. He immediately relaxed.

The first mate thrust a sheet of paper across the table:

"Here, lieutenant, read this and sign it, you're a member of our committee."

What committee, he wondered? It was a document writing off forty litres of pure alcohol. A quarter of a year's worth. Out of which, three litres were allegedly given personally to him, lieutenant Petrukhin. He hadn't so much as got a glimpse of it. It's obvious. They've consumed the whole lot without us.

Trying not to look at the first mate's heavy face, he signed the document. Afterwards, one more was thrust under his nose. About the use of provisions. He'd heard rumours about ninety kilograms of butter which had gone missing but here all was as smooth as in a fairytale. Last time he was on watch, he saw a quartermaster making several trips off the ship, carrying away bags which contained something so similar to tin cans that he found it painful to watch. He carried them off and put them in a mini-truck. To hell with them! Let them choke on it. In the end, what happens to the supplies department isn't for him to worry about. It looks good in the document. True, the sailors have only had margarine instead of butter and the morning portions of it have been melting; and instead of meat, it's some hairy scraps floating in the pot but, on this bloody ship, there is after all a commander, his first mate and the political officer (here's his signature, by the way). What, do you need more than anyone else? Just forget it… forget the whole thing. What else? A document discharging ammunitions. Half a year's worth – one hundred and fifty signalling flares! That must have been quite a bang! Why so many? Perhaps they were shooting each other?!

"Come on, now, lieutenant, sign it quickly. Why are you reading it over for the tenth time? Don't worry, I've checked it myself. You understand – we don't have time to gather you all. Time is of the essence."

Fine. The weapons? Well, they're counted every day. Where could they go? The ammunitions? Well, there were fire drills. Anyone can confirm that. And if some inspection happens to come – you can always say that at the time of last checking everything was there. Fine.

The first mate puts the papers into his desk and pulls out yet another.

"Here, another one."

It was to discharge one of two new nautical binoculars that had come in two days ago. That's why this document had been drawn up. And here's the administrative report attached to the document: the sailor Kukin, a signalman, dropped it over board; the strap broke and all efforts to save the military property were in vain. The officer of the watch is to get a "severe reprimand"; Kukin to be given his deserts up to his ears, the rest – to be reprimanded, and the binoculars are to be written off as the weather conditions were, let's be honest, stormy, not far short of all-out war-time conditions, so really – thank God nobody was killed in it.

The first mate feels it's necessary to explain:

"Our admiral is turning fifty. You understand, we need to give him a present. These binoculars were issued to us on condition that we only discharged one pair for use. Well, you lieutenant, know how things work around here already. Any questions? No? Good man," the paper goes into his desk. "Well, lieutenant, bring over your bottle."

He left the first mate puzzled: what does he mean, my bottle? But then the penny dropped: he wants to pour me some of that pure alcohol.

He found a bottle in the bags rack.

"May I? Here, comrade captain second grade."

The first mate takes the bottle and begins the holy rite: he opens the door of the cupboard and extracts a container. A twenty-litre container. Then other things appear: a funnel and some tubing. One end of the tubing disappears into the container while the other goes into the mouth of the first mate. He's going to suck it. The first mate's face is straining with effort, he goes bright

SEA STORIES | 103

red, he screws up his eyes with zeal – the first mate sucks hard and – phew, the sod! – a silver stream of pure alcohol starts shooting into the bottle.

The first mate wrinkles his face – a drop got into his windpipe, he's coughing and croaking syphilitically:

"That's how we're poisoning ourselves… every day… fuck it… fucking… went right down to my core." The first mate had tears in his eyes, he drank some water and sighed with relief. "Ugh, shit, I'll end up dying here with you lot. Here, lieutenant, next time you'll suck it yourself. And now hide it, so no one sees it…"

Evening was falling. "The heavenly stars, the faraway stars…" The town was glittering in the distance. There was a row of lights along the water. People were sitting now in their warm flats… Shit…

He called the messenger. A young one arrived: puny, a blank stare, puffy lips, dirty hands, and he's stinking, his overcoat burnt through in at least ten places, trousers covered in patches, beat-up shoes, some sort of moron: he came in and said nothing.

"Why aren't you saying anything, you choleric corpse, what's your message?"

"The sailor, Kukin, has arrived, as you ordered."

"A-ah, you old friend. Are you an old friend? Eh? What trash they draft into the navy…"

This was the one who had drowned the binoculars in accordance with the official report. Someone like him can easily drown his own head, no sweat. And tomorrow they'll give the binoculars "To the great leader of the navy. From his loving subordinates." And he'll accept it, without even asking where it came from. Everyone understands. The tarts. You're stuck here, and there's not a single human being around, they're all bastards. And this one is standing here like a dimwit. Ears sticking out, mug covered in spots. Look at this scarecrow. White eyelashes like on a pig. And his cap's two sizes too big, knocking around on his head like a used condom. Can you even call him a human?

"Well, well, you bog's curse, come nearer. Do you want a punch in the face?"

The sailor came nearer, hesitating along the way. He's afraid. At least someone on the ship is afraid of you. He's afraid – it means he respects you.

"You must look me in the eyes when you're receiving orders! Into my eyes!"

Pushes up his chin.

"Maybe you're unhappy about something? Eh? What could you be unhappy about, putrid virus? So, you rotten rookie, on the double, find me the political officer and tell him to come over here. I'm giving you five minutes."

Fifteen minutes later, the youngest and the lowest of the boat's political crew, was sitting next to him in the cabin.

The door's locked, the porthole bolted and curtain drawn; on the table – a bottle (the same one), some bread, a couple of tins of food, a heavy metal teapot from the galley with dark, hot tea (one has friends in the galley, too).

"Where's this from?" the political officer looked sideways at the bottle.

Carelessly:

"They give it out for cleaning. It's by the rules."

"You live well," he sighs, "but they don't give me any, there's nothing to clean."

"It's fine, you'll grow up, become a mate, and you'll get some yourself. For cleaning. You'll be cleaning your subordinates'…"

After the first glass, the political officer became emotional and related how the first mate had yelled at him today in front of the sailors for not filling in the registration forms. They fell silent and picked at the tins. Then they were off again, discussing life in the navy, always life in the navy…

And the first mate was so friendly today. With the documents. He needed the binoculars. When they need something, they're as sweet as…

They finished the bottle. Then tea and then the political officer went off to get some sleep.

He called for the messenger. He waited – but no one came. Where is he loafing around, he wondered? He called again and was told: he's already left.

"What d'you mean 'he's left'? Where's he gone? What are you soiling my brains for?"

His shift is over. Or he'd have been here a long time ago.

The messenger came in.

"Kukin, you bastard, where've you been, moron? How dare you present yourself before an officer dressed in that despicable way? Got no one to look after you, is that it? What are you muttering there? Come closer. Where were you?"

The sailor stays silent. He comes over timidly. He stands head forward so that he could easily recoil.

His terror is annoying, just annoying.

"Shut the door!" He shuts it.

"And take off your belt."

He takes it off. His trousers fall down and he tries to keep them up.

"Give it here!" The lieutenant bends the boy over, shoves his shaven, feeble head between his knees and – in a frenzy – whips him on his stuck-out buttocks. The boy doesn't resist. Because he's cattle, cattle!

"And now clean the place!"

He crawls around, cleaning. It takes ten minutes.

"Finished?"

"Yes, Sir!"

"Get lost!"

HOW YOU LOSE YOUR MIND

We were in the middle of this transfer-reception business. You don't understand? Well, our crew was receiving this submarine from the Dolgushin crew. The job was urgent: a week later we were to go on a patrol on this sub.

And so that we should get the job done quickly, without any meanderings, they put us all onboard – both crews – and towed us away from the shore. We put down the anchor and began the transfer-reception.

In as much as everyone wanted to go home, and as per instructions, that is, without any meanderings, we completed the process in just four hours.

Our commander was very keen to get back to the base to have enough time for his "nightcap". A "nightcap" is a one-litre swill before bedtime: our commander only drank at the base.

We set off for the base but they wouldn't let us land – the base didn't give the "okay".

At 18 hundred hours they didn't give the okay, and at 20 hundred hours they didn't give it, and at 21 hundred hours they didn't give it – they didn't have a tugboat.

At 22 hundred hours the commander lost his patience and decided to go back to the base independently – without a tugboat.

We had no sooner set off than the observation and communication posts – those enemies of the human race – reported on us to the command.

They panicked up above and began yelling:

"Vessel eight hundred and fifty five! Where are you going?"

"Where, where… on a summer holiday, that's where. We're going back to base, dammit!"

The commander hissed to the radio operators:

"Silence! Don't answer them, we'll deal with them later!"

Well, fine. We move independently and finally arrive in the base.

The operations officer, holding his breath, is observing us, wondering how these idiots are going to moor without a tugboat.

"Not to worry," the commander said on the bridge, "we'll moor somehow…"

And we began to moor "somehow"… with the help of appropriate interjections, alone, in other words with just our diesel engine: our boat's sailing effect is considerable, the engine was thrashing, it couldn't cope; the boat was being carried off; the commander kept on smoking and observing as we were carried towards the diesel boats: there were three of them there, moored on the left side of the wharf; the right side of the wharf was empty but on the left three diesel boats protruded and we were being dragged by the wind right towards them, and we were slamming our feet on the brakes – all to no avail.

The guys on the diesel boats noticed all of this: they

climbed up to the upper deck and stood there wondering when we'd ram into them. These diesels were also due to go on patrol the following week. The horror! We were going to bust them up, any minute now! A hundred metres was left… fifty… twenty five… and we kept being carried along…

The commander's pouring with sweat like a woman in labour, he's wringing his hands and lamenting:

"That's it… that's it… they'll throw me out of the navy… the academy won't take me… they'll take me to court… send me to camp… tree-felling… in stripy overalls…"

But then suddenly the boat stalled on the spot… floating… twelve metres to the diesels…

"Go back," stutters the commander in his crazed state, "back, come on now, my dear… come on… quietly… come on, dear… well… my dear, well… come on…"

And the boat stopped for some reason, and – like a miracle – turned around one centimetre after the next, dragging along, at first forward, then it stopped and it carried on and pushed up against the wharf. That's it! It's landed!

"Well!" said the commander, wiping away his sweat. "Well, really… that's really, bloody… my throat's all knotted up… knock me over sideways… Really… That's how you can lose your mind… We made it… Well I never… Can't get my breath back… Well, I, you know… almost pissed in my pants… all over myself… y-e-sssss….

I'll go and take something for my chest. My heart's pounding away like mad…"

Our commander went and took something for his chest. A one-litre swill.

THE PERSON IN RESERVE

If your eyes are tired, turn them towards captain first grade Platonov. Your eyes can rest on him. He's a chummy little old man in glasses; he has a childish, mischievous expression on his face with a sly smile, especially if he's sitting in the garden reading the national papers. Not in a million years would you guess that he's a legendary submariner, an internationally known commander for his cunning manoeuvres, his daring decisions and his stunning escapades on land.

Once, at a health resort, he was at a loss for what to do, so he got well and truly drunk and decided to bathe in his birthday suit having undressed right there on the town beach. So they grabbed him, tied him up, arms behind his back, knocked him around the head and carried him off to the commandant's office from where he ran away, breaking a board in the toilet. But, of course, he rarely got drunk like that.

One day, on a training mission, his boat surfaced to cruise level while a helicopter of unknown nationality hovered in the air, right above his sub's rocket deck.

Helicopters don't hover above submarines often enough for Platonov to figure out their identification.

"Americans, probably", Platonov decided, "but maybe they're English. It must be their Sea King."

So he sent everyone down below while he himself climbed into the deck house, took off his trousers and, bending over, showed his bluish bottom to world imperialism. Grabbing his buttocks, he also bent over several times, energetically, for an explosion, to acquaint his overseas colleagues with his inner uniqueness.

While he was straining away like this, the annoyed voice of the Commander of the Northern Fleet bellowed out:

"Hey! Pla-to-nov! Pla-to-nov! Put on your trousers! And for ignorance of the Russian-made military equipment you'll get a bad mark. Hand in your test report on tactics to me personally."

One day this legendary personage asked on a briefing before the patrol: "Comrade commander, how should we react on receiving a distress signal from a foreign vessel?"

"Tell them to get lost, got it?" said the commander.

"Got it, Sir!" said Platonov. It turned out to be a prophetic question. At the end of the patrol, on their way back to the base, there was an SOS signal coming up; a Norwegian bulk carrier was drowning – there was a fire onboard and water leaking in.

The submarine came to the surface and went over to the bulk carrier. The sub's emergency crew jumped off the boat. They put out the fire, started up the engine, filled in the holes, re-stocked their fuel and … bye-bye.

Arriving back at the base, Platonov reported the incident.

"Ahhhhh!" yelled the chiefs. "It's a military mission! Secrecy of position! "D minus!" They prepared documents to discharge him into the reserves.

But the Norwegian sailors, knowing how things work in our navy, got busy at their end and requested an award for the commander of submarine "K-420", captain first grade Platonov, for his rescue operation.

"We've already rewarded him," replied our officials.

"He's been rewarded already," they assured the Norwegian naval attaché.

"Well, then send us written confirmation that you've rewarded him and we'll interview him later, too," said the Norwegians, not giving in.

The affair had taken an international turn. Finally, they had to keep him in the ranks: they gave him an official reprimand and at the same time honoured him with some sort of a medal.

And yet the Norwegians didn't calm down until their government had also dug up a Norwegian decoration for him.

Taking a vacation after all this at a health resort in the Crimea, Platonov had some sort of medicinal bath treatment for the first time in his life. Suddenly he became aware with a pleasant sense of surprise that his health was an object of interest: a bloke in a white gown came over, took his pulse and asked how he was feeling.

After the medical personnel had left, Platonov got out of the bath, put a white gown on himself – it was hanging there on a hook – and dressed the same way (the gown reaching to the floor), and with a serious mug, went around all the cabins and checked all the women's pulses and asked how they were feeling. The ladies were delighted with such frequent visitation by medical personnel.

The wife of the captain came to her senses first: she'd already seen this gnome somewhere; and when they met at the canteen, then at last nothing could stop Platonov from being sent into the reserves.

HUSH, LITTLE ONE

You mustn't take life in the navy too seriously or you'll end up climbing the walls. And you mustn't take your boss too seriously either. He's not screaming at you for any particular reason, it's just because he's your boss: his status requires it. He can't help it. He's screaming at you and you're standing there, thinking:

"If pigs could fly… a pig would fly right over you, my good fellow, and the pig would look down at you and do a huge …". The main thing is not to smile at any point or your boss will have an apoplectic fit, choke and die, and they'll have to give you a new boss.

So it's best not to think of anything during a ticking-off, just turn yourself off: as soon as he's catapulted himself over to your body, you go – zip, and your consciousness is switched off. And then you can start dreaming: you can stand there, dreaming…

"CDP!" CDP is the Central Dosimeter Post.

"It's the CDP!"

Central command is calling, god dammit!

"Is the head of the chemical department there?"

"Yes, Sir."

"You're to report to the central post."

That's always the way: your boss will turn up if you so much as think about him. Well, you'd better relax now, assume an expression of fear mixed with the tortured look of a girl-captive.

"Come here!… Closer!… Stop trembling! Who are you?! I'm asking you, who the hell are you? Who do you take me for? Who'd'you take me for?! Answer me! Who?!!"

Father Christmas, I say to myself.

"Why didn't you report it?! Why, I'm asking you? Why?!!"

Oh dear! What's he talking about?

"Wake up, you're in a stupor! I'm asking you: where is it? Where?!"

There is such a slew of funny replies to his "where?" you can't believe it. But the main thing is to make your face a portrait of fear – of the reprimand, of an unwanted transfer, of everything. Make the fear visible. But you need to block what's going on inside your brain. That's how we spend our time now – and there's all the time in the world to practice. The "blocking" is often beautiful. Some people manage it so well that the only difficulty is returning to the surprising surface world. For example, he's started giving you a dressing-down and you imagine a ripe watermelon. A huge one. The bum needs to be small, I mean the watermelon's bum, and the top part is large. One touch and it bursts. And we bite into it. And it runs down our hands. Now you can take a little look at what he's up to.

"When?! When?! When did this happen?!"

Oh dear, what's going on here? Oh dear, so much salivating.

"… an order! You won't leave the ship! You'll die here!!! Yes! That'll teach you!"

I wonder what…?

"I'm going to make you scream!"

Oh, that…

"And how!! And eat metal! Here's to your dry land, ha!"

Oh dear, what indecent gestures.

"Here's to your transfer! Here's… to you… in your mouth… an umbrella handle! Suck it off!!!"

Really, what sort of language is that! Look, who are you working for? What sort of college did his mother send him to?"

"I forbid you to leave the ship forever! You'll rot right here! SO THERE! Why are you turning up your nose? Why are you... report to me every day! Do you hear? Every single day on God's earth!"

Hush, little one, what are you howling for, huh?

"... and your papers... today! From my assistant! You will bring everything to me personally! So there... yes... and you thought... we will start a new life! You're not transferring anywhere! You'll rot here! We'll rot together! And when you crawl over to me... well then..."

Well, what wild dreams we entertain.

"Yes, yes, yes! Then we'll see! GET O-OUT!"

Oh, what a gaping mouth! Like a black hole. I wish it were big enough for them all to disappear into. I move slowly along the gangway – "born to crawl, he can't fly". How I wish I could fly. Like a butterfly, like a Malachite butterfly! Through the fields. Off into the horizon. Into the blue sky. Far, far away. A brainless little head. With nothing in it at all. Otherwise, why would we have ended up here, kissing clumps of earth... Now, we're in for it...

THE HOMELESS

(a gathering of officers who don't have a place to live; an abbreviated account)

The officers who don't have a place to live have been

gathered in the assembly hall for the completion of a legal procedure. The admiral comes in. The command is given: "Comrade officers…"

It is drowned out by the noise of chairs standing up. The admiral:

"Comrade officers…" (The noise of chairs sitting down.)

Next is the admiral's examination of the hall (the admiral makes it look as if he's inspecting the Borodino battle field), then:

"You!" (Somewhere in the depths, maybe into the field.) "You! You there! Yes… yes you! No, not you! Sit down! You! Yes, you, the red head, stand up! Why do you look like that… is this the way to attend a meeting? … D-o-n't look at yourself as if you've only just seen yourself. Why haven't you had your hair cut? What? And where are your medals? What're you looking at your chest for? I'm asking you why you've only got one medal? Where are the rest? What ship are you from? It's an outrage! Where are your bosses? … Is that your officer? Eh? What, don't you recognise your officer? What? He's from the reserves? Well, who cares that he's from the reserves? Does that mean he's not an officer? Or doesn't he have anyone to beat sense into him? … Sort this all out… Then report to me afterwards… I said report to me *afterwards*… and on everybody else … alphabetically by surname… Well, we'll get onto that later… I can see you don't understand… After the meeting has been dismissed… I'll get it into your head if you don't understand. So anyway! Comrades! What have we all come here for really? Yes! So we can get this situation with apartments sorted out… A complicated question… the situation's not simple… there's a lack of supply… pipes… complicated obstacles… We weren't given the promised (lots and lots of figures) square metres… But! We – are – officers!" (For fuck's sake!) We all knew what we were getting into! (Cut your mother in half!) Burdens and sacrifices! (Ugh, ugh!) To bear it all stoically! (Ugh, UGH!) And your wives mustn't come anymore! (So there…) The army's not a kindergarten… So! About the apartments… it should all be clear by now! There aren't any apartments and there won't be any… in the near future… But! … Here's a waiting list… Everyone is to put down the surnames of their officers… So that no one will be forgotten! Other than the apartments, are there any questions for me? No? Right, then you're all dismissed. The commanders please stay behind."

"Comrade officers…" The noise of chairs standing up.

I CAN STILL…

I can still poison a well, release rabid squirrels on an enemy, put on my gas mask in two seconds.

I can start an installation filled with lethal gases,

distinguish (by sight and by smell) adamsite from phosgene, mustard gas from soman, CS gas and chloropicrin.

I know all sorts of "characteristics", "decisive factors" and "means".

I can do without sleep for three days, or wake up every other hour, or sleep sitting, standing; and do that for ten days in a row.

I can not drink, as easily as not eat, as easily as running or do a 'forward-march' for twenty four kilometres, in full marching gear, in fulfilment of the order "Gas!", in other words in a gas-mask and in protective clothing; just occasionally I'll need to empty the sweat from underneath the gas-mask – our masks aren't designed for the sweat to be emptied automatically – especially if so much has gathered that it begins to squelch everywhere and rise up into my nostrils.

I see well at night, I can bear the freezing cold and heat. I'm not afraid if my teeth become wobbly and my gums start hurting and bleeding if I press them with my tongue. I know what to do.

I know which herbs and leaves are edible; I know that if you chew for long enough, even reindeer moss is digestible.

I can swim – in calm or in a storm, with the current or against it, in flippers or without flippers, in a heated wetsuit or without a wetsuit. I can swim either way for a long time. I can be separated from my family for several months, I can step forward "for the defence of the homeland", get ready, having dropped everything, and then fly off the devil alone knows where. I can live with ten people in a room, without heating, with wives – my own and other people's – warming up under the blanket with our own breathing, dressed in diving suits as jumpers.

I can shoot in the heat, when the barrel is red hot, and in the cold, when your fingers stick to the metal.

I can set up machine guns on the roof of a house so I could shoot out the whole block, I can come up with a rescue plan or a plan of attack, I can throw a grenade or kill a person with one blow – people are so easy to kill.

I can still do all of that...

I STILL REMEMBER...

I still remember that nuclear submarines can travel under water for one hundred and twenty days, or even longer – if they have enough food; and if the refrigeration stops working, then you need to eat the meat to start with – in huge chunks for breakfast, lunch and dinner, after soaking it in mustard for a day, and then – the tinned food: you can hang on for many days thanks to tinned food. And then the grains and dry bread come into play – you can hold on till you get to shore. And when you arrive you have a day or two to stock up and again they send you out to sea on an equally long patrol.

I remember my compartment and all the equipment

in it; I shut my eyes – and it's all there in front of me, and I can remember all the other compartments, too. I can even travel around them in my mind. I remember where the pipelines are, and where they lead to, where the hatches are positioned, the speedometer, the railings, the airlocking doors. I know how many steps to reach them if you screw up your eyes, hold your breath, if the place is filled with smoke, and you're feeling your way blindly from one airlocking door to the next.

I remember how the body of the boat creaks in a sudden dive and how it creaks when the boat falls to the very depths; when it goes down like a rock, then it's impossible to open the door to the command cabin because the hulk is pressed against the depths and the door is squeezed in around its perimeter. That can happen, too, at the "jamming of the large stern rudder in a dive". Then the boat rushes down, nose-first, and it can be squashed at the bottom, then nobody can do anything, so they shout from the central post – "Bubble in the nose! Full speed backwards!" and whoever is still standing, dashes off to the bow headlong through the flying boxes.

I remember that the maximal differential balance is 30 degrees and how the boat hovers at that, and everyone's eyes jump up into their foreheads and everything is damp to your pants, and there's no air in your lungs, and there's such silence onboard you can hear the water splashing around the light hulk, and then the boat shivers and "settles", and you "settle" with the boat, and inside it's as if a string has broken, and your legs aren't what they used to be – they won't hold you, and you sit down on anything you can find and you sit – not moving a muscle, and then you are filled with such joy that you laugh and laugh…

I know that every half hour the watch must go around the compartment and report to the central post; I know that if anything happens you mustn't step out of your compartment, you must stay in it, shut the airtight door and do your best to stay alive; and if that "something" happens in the compartment next to yours and they're jumping up and down trying to get to yours, crazed, shaking, then it's your holy duty to drive them back with kicks, lock the door with the bolt – let them fight.

And I also know that boats sometimes perish from a trifling fire when there's been a tiny little spark but they've been slow to deal with it – and suddenly everything's burning, and they bring a fire-extinguisher from the central post, but they get confused and give it to the wrong compartment, and people start suffocating in there, and they give high pressure air to the one which is burning up – also by mistake, of course, and for some reason the fuel tanks are squashed and they blaze up like an open-hearth fire and the men – amazingly, they're still alive – run like mad, you won't be able to hold them back anymore; and something all around is falling, falling, cracking, exploding, collapsing, shifting, and a fiery whirlwind is travelling along the corridors, and men are burning up, crackling, like straw, and here bulkhead stuffing boxes of a demagnetising device have burnt to ashes, and the compartment is filling with water, and through the ventilation shafts and through some other way – the devil only knows which one – the neighbouring cabin is filling up with water, and in the central post, they're still trying to get the right differential, still plugging away at the differential but can't seem to get the right differential for the life of them…

THINGS YOU CAN DO TO AN OFFICER

You can easily stop an officer from being promoted to the next rank or office, or you can stop him receiving a medal, which he basically deserves. This is to make him serve better, you understand.

Alternatively, don't stop his promotion. Just retain him in the navy for a while, for an extra period of time – and it's best not to specify how long so he really feels the time passing.

You can refuse to let an officer enrol in the naval academy or any sort of refresher course for officers. By all means, let him enrol if you will, but only on the last day, when it's too late. There's a higher purpose to all of this: it's so he should feel, you know, *really* understand, so his tiny little brain finally comprehends… that things can't really go his way.

You can prevent him from going ashore, assuming he's a naval officer, or you can grant him some personal "org. time": a sort of probation for him to get it together. You can also let him ashore for such small nuggets of time that he finally gets it: he's going to have to behave himself from now on.

Or you can send him somewhere on an assignment that pays much less, where he won't get the northern allowance. You can extend his active service for another term, or a third or even a forth. Or you can keep sending him out to sea, to the artillery testing grounds, to do military surveillance, to some godforsaken hell-hole, and that's if he's lucky. And don't provide him with a flat so his wife has to leave the garrison... Because who's going to renew her residence permit when her husband's so far away?

Or you can decide to give him a flat after all. "There you go... now, who says we don't look after you?" Don't give it to him immediately, though, wait at least five years – maybe eight or fifteen, maybe even eighteen – let him serve a bit longer, give the man a chance to prove himself.

You can also reprimand the bastard or give him a warning followed by a severe warning, and finally some sort of "official warning about the non-conformity of his fulfilment of service". Announce it and then just sit back and watch how he reacts. Or you can arrange things so he never gets another job despite ten years of "irre-proachable service" and he'll rot in the navy, taking test after test (after test, after test) for the "right to independent authority".

You can start monitoring every step he takes, not just aboard ship but in his private life, too. You can organise sudden checks for any "missing" items, commissions, training exercises, presentations and alarms.

Or you can refuse to give him a reference or "letter of recommendation". You can, of course, decide to give him this letter of recommendation after all, but of the sort that he'll end up spitting out bile for a long time afterwards when he reads it.

Or you can make sure he doesn't get his annual pay increase and only a fraction, or perhaps none, of his bonus.

You can leave him no annual leave, or leave him some leave but at a time of year when no normal person would take a holiday. Or you sign all the papers for his leave but you take his plane ticket and stick it in a safe somewhere, while you yourself go off for a week's holiday – he can rush about in a panic, but it won't help.

Or you can make him work through his holiday, checking that he's there every single day – you can even arrange for him to report to you hourly about his whereabouts.

Or, come to think of it, you can lock him up, that son of a bitch, put him in the cooler! Um, the guard house, I mean... And only let him out of there to the open sea! Only to the open sea!

Or you can transfer him to the reserves when he really doesn't want that or, on the contrary, refuse to transfer him when his soul aches for the reserves. Let him fret about it, let him foam at the mouth.

Or you can cut his pension to far less than he'd hoped for, or miscalculate how many years he's served when he's about to retire – let him suffer; or pay out his salary a day before the full month is up or a day before the full year, so he's one day short of earning his full pension.

So basically, there are a million and one things you can do to an officer! There are so many things you can do! There are so many things to try! ... So many that my chest swells with excitement and I start to feel dizzy with anticipation.

"The entire army system of relationships beyond the military manual is built on daily humiliation, both physical and moral which amounts to savagery."

Alexander Terekhov

Alexander Terekhov
ARMY STORIES
From *Memoirs of my Army Stint*

translated by Ben Hooson

THE STORY OF LANCE-CORPORAL RASKOLNIKOV
Related by Junior Sergeant Maltsev

I'm not suffering.

I have a nice, quiet life. I sleep well, my appetite is healthy and I'm OK in every way. As far as I'm concerned everything is simple. But, for all my nonchalance, I'd like to live better – calmer, I suppose... Sometimes, before sleep, when the body melts, becomes weightless, insignificant, then my soul stirs within, swells – I feel it like the wide, hot palm of my hand in the sun, I feel it clearly, to the last bend on my finger, to the tiniest splinter piercing my skin...

I can hardly remember the old fences, that my arms leant on to heave my body somewhere – into a garden, onto grass – and I can't go climbing into somebody else's garden any more, I have no desire to. There are only splinters and voices with them, faces and something else, like wind perhaps, like its vague, uncertain gusts, and all this doesn't flow, and therefore doesn't end, but just – gets in the way somehow: faces, voices, wind...

And then, in the evenings, I fall against the table and my hand thoughtlessly gives birth to words, strings them into lines. I hem myself in with them, I don't like plain white, I squeeze myself out, and nothing else is of any concern to me – this is mine, after this I feel better. After shedding this I can age more easily and calmly observe the wrinkles and irreversible changes to my face. For that purpose alone – here is my truth.

The story of lance-corporal Raskolnikov isn't a curious tale or some events of general interest – it is what I want to be free of.

I remembered all this after our stupid meeting at the start of July this year. It was in Moscow, I had spent all day running round the shops and when there was only an hour to the train I was queuing for sausage at a little shop near the Paveletsky Station. The queue was pestered by flies and heat. Fans were waving their blades weakly on the ceiling, but gave no relief; the windows had been flung wide open.

I was in a hurry so I was looking at the clock on a lamppost, which I could see straight out of the window.

A tall, thin young man in glasses was standing under the clock, near the tram stop, fiddling with a bouquet of flowers – three tulips, I think. I was thinking about my wife – we were expecting our second child, so I thought about flowers too, and about what sort of a girl that young man was waiting for. Then he saw his girl. I knew that, because he grabbed his glasses and shoved them in his pocket. And I recognised him at once – it was Raskolnikov. He didn't use to wear glasses and I didn't notice before that he had fine auburn hair.

I turned to the old woman whose stomach was pressing into my back, said to her "I'll be back", and went slowly out onto the street. Over the road, Raskolnikov was giving the flowers to his girl – I couldn't remember her afterwards. She kissed him on the cheek. I didn't want to go up to him, but it was important to me that he saw me, so I whistled loud, putting the palms of my hands on the back of my neck.

Raskolnikov turned his head, waited for the tram between us to go past, and only then screwed up his eyes and let go of his girl's hand. Now he had recognised me too, and even though he couldn't see every bit of the expression on my face, because of his short sightedness, he understood that I saw him clearly. He looked in my direction calmly and openly, without moving. And so we meet again, Raskolnikov.

He hurriedly said something to his girlfriend – I'd like to know what he said! It was strange: I wanted to see his face at the precise moment when he understood that I was who I was, when everything suddenly came back to him, but now I had seen it I didn't know if his calmness pleased me or not.

He thought I would come over. He was probably thinking how he would answer me and what I would say then. He would probably have stood like that a whole hour, but I was in a hurry, so I turned and went back for my sausage, my mind vacant. When I looked out of the window they were already turning the corner. Raskolnikov's back was straight. Nothing had happened.

I'd been called up in my third year at polytechnic. I still dreamt of making rockets, I thought I was more grown-up and serious than the kids from technical school, with their dyed hair and cheap chains round their neck, so I kept myself to myself at the transit camp, which just made it all sadder. There was a drunken crowd around the office. People were scrambling up trees, pulling up frantic women behind them, trying to get over the fence. A fat warrant officer was strolling up and down by the fence, slashing at the most daring with a bunch of nettles, making them squeal and swear at him from the trees.

After a couple of days they brought some lads from Sverdlovsk and a smiling boy, Serioga Barintsov, settled on the bunk opposite mine. It turned out that he'd been at polytechnic too, but was expelled in the second year for drinking, then worked as a taxi driver till he got called up. Like me, he had no one to see him off, so we shared our boredom, slouched round the transit camp, set fire to rubbish and old leaves, told each other jokes before bed – that made it easier to go to sleep, stopped us from crying.

We were two days on the train to where we would start our service. It was a horrible trip – makes me sick to think of it. Everyone was drunk, and you couldn't breathe in the lobby between carriages for the rancid smell of puke. The conductresses had no bed sheets, but they had cheap vodka for sale. I didn't overdo the drinking and Barintsov didn't get carried away either – at least he didn't buy his own, he held onto his money.

On the second night I was woken by a kick in the side. Three tech boys, stoned with drink, asked for money, they were desperate for more drink. The carriage was dead quiet: everyone was asleep. I tried to turn it into a joke but one of them showed me a knife in his pocket. I was just about to reach for the money when Serioga jumped down and swore at them at the top of his voice to get out of here and let him sleep. The lads scurried away and turned in – even the conductress came along like a sleepy rat to see what was the matter. I stayed awake, worried about the knife, but in the morning everybody laughed about it, even the tech boys.

Barintsov was what you call sussed. He was the first to find out where they were taking us, what they would train us as. He was the only one who kept his provisions untouched, and we had midnight feasts for the first three days of training when the others listened with envy to their neighbours' chewing and remembered with anguish every morsel they'd left uneaten on the train. The army cabbage soup and watery potatoes with black lumps still stuck in our throats.

Barintsov didn't blab about the women he'd had, like all the others did, he didn't tell dirty jokes, he liked most to sleep and eat, and everyone took a liking to him. I was even a bit proud of him, like an elder brother. Maybe he felt that and took me under his wing.

They put us in the first platoon, where at the end of the week a down-to-earth miner called Petrenko was appointed as the senior man. After about three weeks, when it started getting colder, the sergeant-major took us to the stores for greatcoats. The platoon lined up breathing in the back of each others' necks, already in their coats, and the sergeant-major bit his lip measuring distance from the ground to the bottom of the coats to make sure it matched regulations. To make life easier for himself he called us all "Vasya", except the lads from Central Asia, whom he called "asiatics". He gave me an order:

"Right, Vasya, swap your coat with this Vasya."

I went to one side with a shaven-headed lad with big, frightened eyes. He had such a soft face. My coat was just right for him, but his was too long for me.

"Never mind, we'll find you one." The sergeant-major waved his hand. "You go and sign for it. Surname…"

"Raskolknikov," the boy said, touching his forehead with his hand.

"What, the murderer?" Petrenko said, writing the names and sizes. "Topping grandma with an axe?"

And that is how we met.

Early on in the training we were always hungry. Barintsov used to imagine before he went to sleep how he'd eat a loaf of bread, a stick of sausage and two litres of berry jam all on his own – he laughed off the hunger.

I found it harder.

I started hating people. I'll hate the soldiers mess of those first days as long as I live: jostling people on the way to the table; anxiously counting how many people there were on the bench so as not to be one too many; the order "Pass it round!" and instantly putting your hand out to be the first, to get the fattest slice of the loaf; the anxious whine with plate extended: "More! That's not enough!" and then racing through the first course to be the first to the ladle and get a serving of the second course that still had meat, not just fat; then get a second helping of the first course, which you couldn't get at once (because you might be too late to get any of the second); then scrape the porridge from the ladle, grab some sugar – two pieces – and straight in your pocket; hold onto the bread with your elbow, taking no notice who had enough and who didn't, and swallow the tea, glancing around to see if anyone left anything, if, maybe, someone hadn't eaten their butter, or the sergeant didn't want his black bread and left it for the rest of us to devour joyously and instantaneously. And every evening, the dribbling whispers about who had got how much, what we'd eat in the future, and how we once ate our fill in the past...

I watched with disgust how I changed, how I, Cadet Maltsev of the Second Platoon, was no longer Oleg Nikolaevich Maltsev, but something else, something more bestial, I suppose. My memory tortured me. I started to keep track of who had given or shared their food with me, and who had eaten when I was next to them and not even thought of sharing. Whenever there was a chance to get into the cafeteria I ate and ate, filled my pockets with sweets, and only shared with people who had shared with me. I learnt to say no easily.

"Maltsev, give us a biscuit."

"Why?"

People noticed this and laughed behind my back, but only Barintsov understood that I was physically unable to grab my portion quicker than the others in the mess, and if I was the last to serve myself that wasn't a protest, it was simply my weakness – I couldn't do otherwise, couldn't open my mouth to ask for more, couldn't hide sugar in my pocket and eat someone else's leftovers. I came to hate people, and – why hide it? – myself. My strange greed was a way of getting back at this animal world, revenge for myself, an effort to lay bare this ugliness through and through.

A couple of things happened towards New Year. At the platoon meeting Barintsov proposed voting for me as Komsomol organizer and the platoon was unanimously in favour. I was happy. I thought this would do more than just keep me afloat – it would raise me.

The other thing that happened was that, on the first night after we got our pay for the first two months of service, someone stole more than a hundred roubles from our platoon, and fifteen of them were mine. I didn't keep money in my soldier's passport, like the others, but in an empty packet of Gillette blades. But that didn't help me – the packet was stolen. Economiçal Barintsov lost thirty at once, and the miner Petrenko lost fifteen, like me. The mood was wretched all round. New Year was coming up and we had no money. The Uzbeks cast grim looks at us and we cast grim looks back, but we had all lost money. More than that, our platoon cast some grim looks at the rest of the company, supposing that a thief wouldn't rob from his own platoon, so he must have come from outside. But how could he have crept across the lighted corridor to another dormitory so the orderly wouldn't see him, even if he was half-asleep.

The sergeant-major got senior members of the platoon together in the quartermaster's store in the morning: Petrenko, Barintsov and myself.

"Whoever guzzles most in the cafeteria is the thief," said Petrenko, who already had a lance-corporal's stripes.

"He won't make straight for the cafeteria," Barintsov disagreed, and his eyes shone cunningly as he made an alternative proposal. "Let's wait a bit and put it around that Maltsev has received a large cash transfer, a hundred roubles, and he puts it in his passport when everyone is looking, and we take it in turns at night…"

"Lads," the sergeant-major said wearily, "that's all kids-in-the-park, ice-cream van stuff. I'll tell you what: think what you like, but don't do anything. The thief will give himself away. He's got to. It'll all come out sooner or later. He's not a real thief – just a hungry idiot."

At the roll call, he said shortly:

"I'll find him, just you wait."

I thought at the time: who could be suffering from hunger more than I was? Not even so much from hunger, as from change of circumstances, from the lack of everything? It seemed they were all taking it about equally and all better than me. I thought first of the Uzbeks – a lot of them hardly spoke Russian so you couldn't know what they were thinking. Serioga tended to agree. "Which one of ours could have done it?" he said. "Raskolnikov is a coward, he wouldn't dare. Korovin was on guard duty that night, and it's not like Petrenko. He's a right guy. So it's not one of them. Probably one of the asiatics."

After the ceremony of taking the military oath we started on specialization with less mindless drill and more quiet study in radio classes with their nervous squeaks of Morse, and we started getting letters from home – in a word, things got easier. On Saturdays the company dragged mattresses and blankets to the sports section and beat the dust out of them with belts and sticks. Over the fence early buses rattled past, street lights whined, bent over the dancing snow flakes, the stars shone and only the very edge of the sky had an unhealthy pallor.

On Saturday Barintsov brought Korovin over to the bar, where I was trouncing my mattress. Korovin was a careful, sly boy, who got a reputation as a layabout later on thanks to his excessive high spirits and relaxed attitude to army life. The sergeant-major once asked Korovin what he'd been doing asleep in an excavator bucket when he was supposed to be on duty at the automotive park, and Korovin answered that he'd had "an attack of moon stroke", for which he got three days in the cooler.

But at the time, Korovin was still a quiet boy. That Saturday he was even sullen.

"Go on then, my lad, tell the Komsomol rep," Barintsov said to him.

"What's there to tell? I woke up at night to go to the loo. I went. I couldn't get back to sleep. Khasanov, sod him, grinds his teeth in his sleep, so I was waiting for him to break them. I'd just lifted my head to wake him, and I saw someone digging around in my vest. I got down and looked in my passport…"

"Why on earth…" Barintsov put in.

"I leafed through it and my twenty-five roubles were still there. He hadn't got to them. I looked to see where he ran – he'd already gone. A bed creaked nearby, but I couldn't tell where… it was black. I went to the loo – no one there either. I asked the orderly – no one had crossed the corridor. So it must be one of ours…"

"But who? Who? Who did he look like? You know your own platoon, don't you?" I got a bit heated, thinking that I'd better show some reaction and not just sit arms folded, being the Komsomol rep.

"Well," Korovin said.

"Think, moo, think," Barintsov insisted. "Who?"

"He looked like Zhusipbekov, I think" Korovin said thoughtfully.

"Zhusipbekov? For sure?" I asked quickly.

"It was dark, but I think it was him."

"You think, you think?" I said angrily. "What am I supposed to do with your think?!"

By the end of the first hour of lessons my head was aching with doubt. But what could I do?

"Oleg, don't be a fool," Serioga said. "No one is saying Zhusipbekov is the thief. But we've got to sort it out. Rumours will get around in any case. Best to avoid rumours, or the asiatics will get nervous. Get everyone together, and we'll say it to each others' faces."

Serioga had got really worked up over this business. I was even surprised how angry he was about losing thirty roubles, although I was sorry to have lost the money too, of course. We'd waited two months for some pay. I wanted to get myself an officer's shirt for parade when we were in the army shop.

It was a good idea to have a meeting. We just stayed in class after study time, except that Serioga called the sergeant-major for some reason. I didn't need the sergeant-major but Serioga maybe thought he'd hold down Zhusipbekov, just in case. He was a tough guy.

"We're having a meeting today," I said. "Korovin, come forward and tell us what you saw that night."

Korovin came out and described what he saw. Adik

Khasanov translated for the Uzbeks. They started chattering in Uzbek, discussing what he'd said.

Zhusipbekov answered them calmly a couple of times, shrugged his shoulders – or maybe not calmly, I couldn't read their faces.

"No, he says it wasn't him," Khasanov translated. "He was asleep."

The rest of the meeting was the same – I was bored to death. Korovin said the same thing again and again. Khasanov translated the response. At least, when you speak the same language, you can make some decent sense of it, feel it, but this was hopeless. I'd done the right thing – we had to sort it out, in any case. The sergeant-major got impatient and stood up. He said:

"Korovin, are you sure you saw the thief?"

"I think so..." Korovin bleated.

I put my hand over my face: to hell with them, let them sort it out.

"Nobody else saw him?"

Silence.

"Nobody?"

Someone said quietly:

"I did."

I looked: Raskolnikov came out from behind the table, and looked unblinking at the sergeant-major. He said again:

"I saw him too. Zhusipbekov was walking around the dorm at night."

Barintsov smiled at me quickly and shook his head, as if to say: how about that? The Uzbeks started chattering, our lot got excited, there was some swearing, but the sergeant-major raised his hand and there was silence.

"All the same", he said, "it doesn't mean anything. People can make mistakes. An innocent man mustn't get punished for someone else. And don't worry, we'll find the thief sooner or later. That's for sure. It's good that we've gone over it, but we can't make a mistake in a thing like this. We'll wait."

And we left it at that.

I hardly knew Raskolnikov. He slept the nights in the platoon but spent whole days in the art department. He didn't draw well himself, but his job was preparing canvases for the artists. He went to the specialisation lessons, but as soon as physical exercise time came round, he was off to the art department. I don't know why, but people thought he was a sneak. That's always the way – someone gets labelled. He is seen once with the political deputy, or there's just something people don't like about him, and they decide: he's the sneak. And it sticks. I was always scared stiff of it. It seemed to me I could get that reputation: I always stood out from the rest, and loners are prime suspects. But, thank God, I was best friends with Serioga, and he dispelled any doubts about me.

Raskolnikov was worse off. He was alone all the time or with the artists – they didn't just draw in the art department, they played cards for fruit juice or for a "civvy" ration from the cafeteria, they read books, even pulled girls in through the window – well, maybe they didn't, but that's what they said in the platoon. Another reason why people decided he was a sneak was that he got a stripe near the end of training – he was made lance-corporal. What for? He wasn't much of a soldier. Not that there's much to sneak about from study time. We were all there together, and nothing much untoward happened. But lance-corporals simply weren't popular all round.

So that's how things were for Raskolnikov.

A couple of weeks after the meeting two soldiers had to be sent off to Aredinsk, way off in Siberia, for service without specialisation. Aredinsk was a name used to frighten layabouts and anyone who didn't try hard enough with the specialisation. It was supposed to be tough there. Zhusipbekov was one of the two who were sent – probably not a random choice. He hadn't studied particularly well. I thought at once that he wouldn't have a nice time there. We were signallers, so the message would travel pretty fast of who Zhusipbekov was and what his story was in training. I had only heard second-hand what life was like in "combat" detachments, but I thought all the same that it wouldn't be easy for him – I wondered if I should have held that meeting or not? But then I thought – not to worry. All our people were happy enough.

The training went like a flash. Everyone was busy exchanging addresses and promising to get together again without fail in such and such a place right after demob, in five years and in ten. And the sergeant-major was counting scarves and socks, boots and certificates under his breath…

They took us out on the parade ground and the battalion commander shouted about how we must live up to the honourable name of our unit, which had trained a good number of heroes. We fairly grew a foot taller hearing that.

Petrenko was made junior sergeant, me and Barintsov were pleased enough to have plain stripes and a "clear conscience", as Serioga added. We were sent off in batches to new units, and a new bunch of conscripts kicked up a shindy in the bathhouse. I felt depressed. Petrenko and Serioga were sent off before me. I knew we'd soon meet again, that we'd be in the same unit, but I felt down all the same – time passes so quickly, I thought…

The day before I was due to go off myself a lance-corporal, who was on duty in the radio room, reported an interesting piece of news with a wry smile: Private Zhusipbekov had hanged himself in Aredinsk. I felt pretty rotten though I didn't know why. What was it to do with me? Nothing! I'd acted as the Komsomol rep, what else could I do? What's the Komsomol rep for? Anyway, no one knew why he'd hanged himself there. Maybe he was unbalanced. Why not? It happens, after all.

But I kept remembering his face as I went through the empty barracks. They all looked the same, but he seemed the most wretched of them – maybe he was from the mountains or something. His mother was probably waiting for him at home. I thought – what would his mother think about a place like Aredinsk? Strange – a person had died; was I sorry for him or not? I suppose not – I hadn't really known him and he didn't speak a word of Russian. The company had broken up – no one would remember Zhusipbekov or find out that he was dead. And when I die won't anyone give a damn? No? No. Of course they won't. You live and you live…

On the last day the sergeant-major made us all knuckle down and mend everything that could be mended and paint everything that could be painted. There were only seven of us left from the whole company. I didn't want to paint – the smell makes be sick at once – so I went off to sew. I went through the barracks looking for holes in mattresses and ragged black-out curtains. I was doing a pillowcase just before lunch; I punched in the feathers with my fist and felt a hard lump. I pulled it out – it was a Gillette packet. I tore it open – there were five roubles.

It was my money. Nobody else in the platoon had blades like that – they all had to make do with Russian brands – Neva and Voskhod. So… and whose bed was it. First, second, third top bunk by the window. No, I couldn't remember. Was it Petrenko?! The bastard! No – he always jumped up from the bottom bunk when the alarm sounded, or was I getting mixed up? No, that's right, from the bottom – he was always mucking around with

Valiakhmetov, going on about mines – and he couldn't have slept at the top anyway, because he was senior in the platoon… So who slept here? Who did the orderly shake by the shoulder every morning at reveille – he used to come in towards morning and say "Get up, get up, Mr Artiste." Artiste? It was Raskolnikov's bed. So that was it. That was it. Zhusipbekov was creeping round the dorm at night – he had seen him, so he said…

I'd never hit a person in my life before. But then, in the empty barracks full of harsh January sunlight I wanted to punch a face, to see bloody blue bruises, smashed teeth, kick into the soft parts of his body through the whines and groans, and say words I'd never said before; turd, swine… God, what came over me?

I went to the Komsomol committee room that evening and held Zhusipbekov's registration card in my hands, looked at his face. I hadn't remembered him like that. And somehow I didn't want to read about him: where he was from, who he was. I searched out Raskolnikov's card. Raskolnikov, Igor Petrovich. Mother a teacher. Father retired due to disability. One younger sister. What else? Where had they sent him? He had gone where I was going. So, so… so what? I searched inside myself for the bitterness I'd felt just two hours ago, but no one in the company was left, they'd all gone, new people will sleep on these beds, a new life will start, the sergeant-major will show them how to make beds and wrap their puttees, and here I stand like an idiot – no one gives a damn about it any more. About what, exactly? Where's the guarantee that the pillow hadn't been swapped. Someone could have put the packet there on purpose – Raskolnikov wasn't such a fool as to forget the money if he had needed it enough to steal it. Nobody could say for sure, nobody could prove it. Nobody could be bothered.

The next day I'd stopped thinking about it.

When I arrived at the combat unit Serioga Barintsov was clearing snow by the barracks, I went up, pleased to see him, hugged him and asked:

"How's it going?" Serioga's lips trembled, his eyes went large and wet. "How… you'll see…" And he quickly bent over the spade so I only saw his back and nothing else. Petrenko came up, as if older, looked around and whispered: "Do it all, but don't wash anyone's socks, even if they beat you hard." "Beat," I repeated, as if it was a foreign word. "What do you mean, 'beat'?"

"They'll beat you every day," Petrenko explained to me with a tired sigh.

"But not often hard – probably only three times in all."

That was the start of our spell as "rookies" – the hardest, dirtiest, most shameful time of my life.

Life turned upside down in a day. In one day I learnt what I could no longer do and what I must do – it was terrifying.

I was still washing the lavatory at one thirty in the morning. Washing it for the third time – they had explained to me twice already that I did it badly, and used fists to make the point. I didn't resist. You wouldn't understand. There's no use trying to understand unless you know – we are animals, not people. Cleaning the floor with a cloth I went round someone's feet again and again, without raising my head. The most important thing is not to make eye contact if you can help it: it irritates them.

Just as I raised my eyes for a second, coming out of the lavatory, I saw Raskolnikov.

Raskolnikov was washing socks. He turned away from me.

"Hello, Raskolnikov," I said to him.

He glanced at me, scared, and barely nodded.

"How's life?" I couldn't make myself smile; there was nothing to smile about for the foreseeable future. I wasn't in a hurry to leave the lavatory, which was safer than this new, brutal barracks with its new smell.

"How's life, Raskolnikov? OK? Are you doing much drawing? Or what are you doing? Washing socks?"

He didn't turn round and said nothing and that made me angry.

"Where are you from?"

"I'm from Moscow."

"Ah, the capital no less. Moscow – capital of our motherland…" I muttered and suddenly remembered: "Raskolnikov, mate, did you know that Zhusipbekov hanged himself?"

He stopped washing, clasped his hands but didn't turn. I started off towards him, my voice rising as I came:

"That's right – the rotten thief Zhusipbekov hanged himself. Private Zhusipbekov the thief. Our comrade in arms, fellow soldier. And I know now perfectly well why he hanged himself there, and you know too… the only thing is whether his mother will understand. You have to imagine how it would be if you hanged yourself and your mother – you do have a mother, yes? – heard about it." I grabbed him by the shoulders and turned him around. He was sobbing silently, mouth open, face twitching.

"You have nothing to say to me about Private Zhusip-bekov? Who got his comeuppance there as a rookie and for stealing from his friends… Nothing to say? Think… you can think, can't you? I often think about it… although I… what is it to me…"

I didn't say anything else – I went to bed.

To be honest, I don't like to think about my time as a rookie. In fact, Petrenko got it worst of all. He was the sergeant and he was strong. So when we became "middlers" after six months I didn't hold it against him for being cruel. I understood Petrenko. I didn't get it so bad from the middlers, but afterwards I sometimes caught myself on the point of meting out a punch.

There's a huge pleasure to it, to have a creature in front of you who would be stronger than you, older or wiser, if he were a person – a creature that trembles and follows your every gesture and expression, stands frozen in dumb pleading and waits with bated breath for whatever you choose to do with him – he doesn't mind anymore, so long as it's quick, though he still hopes inside that you might let him off. And you see right through his little soul, all his vain tricks, his attempts to be nice to you, to distract you, vague hopes that a passing officer or mealtime will help him, and you have him in your hands with an intoxicating sense of your own power: you can hit him hard or not so hard, send him to clean the toilet or buy you a paper or a drink, get him to sing you a song. And the pleasure is all the richer because you can remember yourself in his skin, and you despise him for that as a way of rejecting your own past, you drive yourself away – it is a remarkably bitter-sweet, sickly feeling.

So I didn't blame Petrenko then and don't blame him now for being cruel when he was a middler. I understood.

I got beaten less but they didn't like me. Probably because they couldn't make sense of me. Both the "dads" and middlers felt that I stood apart, even from the other rookies, and that I was thinking about something apart from what I talked about. My constant willingness to forgive and forget, and not to accept my degradation seemed to them like hypocrisy, and they probably reckoned that deep-down I was full of hate – what else could there be inside a rookie in his first three or four months of service when the fool didn't even understand the army. What they enjoyed wasn't to beat me but to humiliate, to make me say something stupid or do something comic, so that they could all stand around me and snigger. When they are together they are clever enough – they understand the nuances.

Rookiedom worked a great change in Serioga Barintsov – he shrivelled up and hung his head. He came in for less trouble than the rest of us, but he still tried his hardest to avoid it and did so in a jerky, nervous way. For some reason, he was particularly frightened. I never saw him smile. He didn't even talk much and concealed our friendship. On the third day, when I still didn't know better, I saw them taking Barintsov into the toilet for a session. I jumped off the bed, dressed as you would be for a session – vest and cotton trousers tucked into boots – and went into the toilet after them. The dads were standing around lazily and Barintsov was in the middle, pale and with a swollen expression.

I went and stood beside him.

"What d'you want?" they asked me. "Nothing special, I'll just stand here with you," I said politely. They gave us both one in the face. The next day they dragged me off for a session. Barintsov stayed in bed. A clever dad came back from the toilet and addressed the sleeping dorm:

"Barintsov, don't you want to do like your friend yesterday?" Barintsov kept on sleeping.

The next day they woke him alone. I didn't get up.

I felt sorry for Serioga, and helped him the best I could, shared my butter with him if they had taken his. I gave him needles, thread, a bit of money. All his good points were still there: common sense, ability to work things out, daring, cunning, but where did his smile go?

They broke Raskolnikov completely. They started with his lance-corporal stripes – unstitched them every night and beat him the next day when he got a reprimand at roll call for not having them. When they took him for a serious session the first time he did what they won't forgive – the wretched weakling gave a feeble thrust in the face of the first one who hit him. After that they woke him every night – by the fifth day he was washing socks for all the dads and had a foul word instead of a name. Even the other rookies weren't allowed to call him by his real name. He went round the camp like he was sick, he kept looking round and hid in the attic, and I thought that the officers surely saw it. We all crept about the place and trembled if someone called our name, but Raskolnikov was obviously torn apart and stamped on. No one would sit next to him in the club to watch a film or in the dorm in the evening – to be near him meant trouble. He wasn't good at our specialisation and there was no job for an artist here, so for a while he was on the kitchen and transport details. And then he suddenly landed the cushiest job in camp – the telephone exchange.

Our garrison had a military college and it had a small telephone exchange. One conscript had to be on duty there at night, to avoid taking on civilians. There were hardly any calls at night and you could do what you wanted: write letters, sleep, smoke, make yourself at home, and then sleep in the day as well: more like heaven than the army. That was the job Raskolnikov got.

But there was one other thing about Raskolnikov: maybe someone brought the story from the training camp, or maybe it was because of the strange decision by camp commanders to put him on telephone duty, but the opinion was that, on top of everything else, Raskolnikov was a sneak. There was no particular proof, except two or three little meetings with the political officer, but nobody really needed proof.

Having made it to the telephone exchange Raskol-nikov stood a little straighter, and looked more collected – he could listen to music there, use a proper toilet, wash and shave at his leisure. The people working at the college addressed him with the formal "You" and gave him extra rations. He probably caught up on his sleep there, because he had a tough time sleeping in the barracks. Everyone made a special effort to knock his bed when they went past, to say something loud right next to his ear, or just to hit him as he lay. I don't know how he stood it: lying motionless on a bed for eight hours with eyes closed, having to listen for the slightest rustle, waiting for a blow, catching the words of passers-by and always seeing them as a threat, and all the while pretending to be asleep so as not to madden people with the idea that he slept at the telephone exchange. I wanted to ask how he stood it, but I couldn't – he was afraid of me and avoided me, although I hadn't shared my thoughts about Zhusipbekov's death with anyone. There was no one to tell. That life was over. All that anyone needed in this life was a good night's sleep and avoiding a punch in the face.

Raskolnikov's weak point was the mess. A person wants to eat, at least from time to time. He had to go there and appear in front of the whole garrison, who all thought he was a sneak. As soon as he showed up they started banging on the table with their spoons, sent him running endlessly to fetch mugs, plates, spoons, made him pour tea and fetch bread, even for the rookies. He had no respect among the rookies – the telephone exchange was a cushy number, and they couldn't forgive him for that.

I felt sorry for Raskolnikov – I always thought that I could have ended up in his place if blind fate had crushed me instead of him. It was as if we had swapped fates instead of coats. As if I saw myself in him, and he was drinking the cup that could have been mine.

What really did for him was relaxation.

Near the time of the first-year order every rookie relaxes. It isn't a protest – there's no hint of protest left in him – but it's the first sign that the end of his time as a rookie is in sight. Some of them start quietly collecting verses and photographs for their future demob album, some of them pump their muscles on the parallel bars, when the dads aren't looking, building up their authority for the next lot of rookies. What Raskolnikov did was to start phoning home every night on the regimental telephone.

His father was an invalid, so he could sleep in the day and talk with his son for nearly an hour by night at government expense. This came out a couple of weeks before the first-year order via the accounts office, which was fed up with paying. Raskolnikov was chucked out of the exchange and our unit was deemed unreliable and deprived of the cushy exchange job altogether.

I thought to myself: never mind, Raskolnikov had already sat out the worst at the exchange. But I was wrong.

A day before the order, our company was woken up in the middle of the night for a check. Four middlers from the second platoon were relaxing in the hostel of the medical college that night. In a couple of days they would be continuing their military service in the Siberian town of Aredinsk where the snow melts only in May. Everyone connected these events with Raskolnikov's return: they decided that he had sneaked on the middlers. The day after the first-year order the new dads called together all the most respected of the new middlers, including Petrenko, and told them there wouldn't be any change in status for Raskolnikov. He would still be treated as a rookie.

The next day sergeant Petrenko sent lance-corporal Raskolnikov to clean the toilet, after half a year sharing a double-decker bunk with him in training.

So ended Raskolnikov's relaxation.

Mine was of a different kind. I fell in love. Every morning a dazzling, long-legged blonde came into work at the military college. She was always on her own, with an aloof, proud expression – and half the garrison watched her go. I watched too – a big-eared rookie with a dirty neck, chewed fingernails and trousers with baggy knees. Several generations of rookies must have fallen in love with her. I wouldn't be surprised.

Love is not really the word in my case: I just watched her and felt better inside, that's all. Seeing her made me breathe differently and demob didn't seem so far away, life seemed simpler and clearer. I sometimes dreamt in the evening of all sorts of foolishness with her – no use hiding it. She was pretty and very, very... that sort of woman, always in tight jeans or a skirt with a suggestive slit, and the way she walked had the duty warrant officer at the checkpoint fairly twisting his head off. Petrenko and Barintsov were the only ones who knew about my penchant. Serioga worked a couple of days cleaning at the college, found out about everything and told me in a whisper that evening that she was called Natasha and married to a major, with no children. Serioga had seen her husband – he wore glasses and was beginning to go bald. What a name – Natasha, Natalia!

Serioga was slowly but surely coming back to life and we started chatting again in the evening, like in training, and just sometimes there would be a happy smile on his face.

"Here's what we'll do," he suggested to me. "We'll buy a bottle, I'll find out when her husband is on 24-hour duty at the college, and we'll go round to her flat.

We'll knock and ask if she'll have a drink with us. And then we'll just see what happens – take it from there. What does she get out of her major? Compared with you – the next Lobachevsky! Just grow your hair a bit, have a wash!"

I giggled and glanced at the dads' beds, out of habit. That wasn't what I wanted at all. Every evening I pictured the same scene to myself and then to Serioga: I am in parade uniform for demob with a chest full of medals – I'll have some medals by that time – I buy twenty-one tulips, meet her in the morning at the camp entrance, and I already have my ticket home. Everyone there is open-mouthed with astonishment. And I say to her "Hello, Natasha, sorry for holding you up, I just wanted to say that I have been serving in this unit for one and a half years and I have been seeing you for one and a half years – at least from time to time. Maybe my looks have said more than they should – sorry for that. All I know is that I won't see you again – I live a long way away, you are seeing me for the first and last time, but I want you to know that for one and a half years you have been a symbol to me of everything beautiful, pure and sacred. Without even knowing it you have helped me to live, to survive. When I saw you, I became a person and I could cope with anything. Thank you." And she would look at me as sad as anything, her mouth would be like a poppy in the wind, and maybe she would think for the first time in her life – had she missed something, had she made a mistake by tearing up the scarlet sails for floor rags, shattering her dreams on the dreary crags of humdrum existence, cutting short her flight, ending the song… in a word, all the rubbish that comes into the head of a rookie when he relaxes. And then she'd probably say something that it was frightening even to think of, or just kiss me quickly, or give me an address to write to in case fate meant us to meet again, and it would be when I would be whoever I would be by then… and so on.

We'd become middlers and we'd relaxed.

We started to smile and live proper lives. Everything would have been fine, except that one night four dads called me to the toilet and said accusingly that they had noticed me being soft on the sneak Raskolnikov. What did I have to say about it?

I had nothing to say about it.

So then they asked me if I wanted to join him so he wouldn't be lonely? I said no. No, I'd done my time and done right. Then they asked maybe I was planning to be soft on rookies generally and not lay a finger on them? No, I said, I wouldn't be soft on recruits, I'd hit them hard… the conversation dragged on and it didn't bode well for me.

At this point Barintsov and Petrenko came into the toilet and stood next to me. The dads asked: what do the middle boys want here? Nothing they said, just a smoke – that's allowed at our stage. Do as you please, damn middlers, the dads said, but make sure that Raskolnikov gets it and there's order in the company. The dads went out and Serioga hugged me and I felt happy because I was no longer a rookie, because everything would be fine for me and there was a woman with the sunlight name of Natasha and soft, sunlight hair, and it was already autumn outside, and generally everything was great.

"Bastards," Petrenko said blowing his moustache (middlers were allowed to have moustaches).

The days went by more quickly. I didn't see much of Raskolnikov, and I didn't want to notice him – there was nothing pleasant in that living reminder of the recent past for me or any of the new middlers.

On the seventh of November there were oranges at lunch in the mess. Serioga woke me that night and told me, first, that he had been made a lance-corporal and, second, that he and Petrenko were the first middlers to get leave; and third, a couple of rookies – Lang and Djikia – had been caught by a hole in the fence with moonshine brought in from outside; and fourth, lance-corporal Raskolnikov had broken his right arm, working out on the bars and was now putting his feet up in the hospital.

"On what bars?" I asked, surprised. "He'd never go to the gym in his life!"

"And fifth," Barintsov bent his little finger, "the dads and middlers reckon the broken arm is a fake. It's just the political deputy trying to save the sneak from a counter blow after the successful operation at the hole in the fence."

I felt miserable. I muttered:

"Christ, how could Raskolnikov know about any hole, he never shows his nose out of the toilet."

"A few specialists are going over to the hospital to hood him and give him a going over," Serioga said, and added as an afterthought. "I just came from the hospital. Sergei the hospital orderly was chatting..."

Barintsov was unaccountably sad and I thought I understood why: leave was a good thing, unheard of happiness for a middler, but what would it be like to come back and know that you had another year still to go?

"So there," Serioga said in a tired voice and sighed with effort, "I had a couple of glasses with the orderly and he told me... because he respects me. He said about Raskolnikov... his first name is Igor, apparently... did you know? I didn't... Anyway, he feels sorry for Igor... Raskolnikov has already been in the hospital a couple of times, do you remember, for Aviation Day? Yes? Well this Sergei got him in. He can. He says that he'd offer to do it for me if I was having a bad time in the company, but he thought I'd be offended, think it below... below my dignity. The political officer is not as dumb as he looks. Turns out, he knows just what's happening to Raskolnikov in the company. That's what Sergei told me, after Raskolnikov – Igor – told him. And the political officer promised to get him moved in a couple of weeks. To another unit, away from us. Somewhere a long way away, where there are no signallers... And when they caught the lads by the fence, Raskolnikov came running to the hospital and told Sergei – I need to break my arm, so I can hide out for two weeks in the hospital…"

Barintsov wasn't very drunk but he told his story with long pauses, breathing through his nose in the silence and grimacing.

"Sergei the orderly did what he could. He injected an anaesthetic and told him to go and break his arm, but to be sure and say nothing if anything went wrong – it's a prison offence. Raskolnikov, the idiot, went and bashed his arm against a corner wall. Bashed it himself. But all he did was give himself a bruise and the arm just bounced off, like a piece of wood. He went to the sports section, put his arm in the bars to break it, but he couldn't. He came back to Sergei, who put him in our ambulance and took him to the first aid station – he has a friend there who agreed to put the arm in plaster, and there you are…"

He looked at his feet and said in a muffled voice:

"And I am going home, I've got leave."

"Yes," I said, coming back to Raskolnikov, "it's just his fate."

"Fate," Serioga repeated after me, and then said strangely, "and what about you, and me?"

He looked at me and I felt I had to give some answer, so I said quickly and with false jollity:

"For us everything is still to come." Barintsov took off his belt and started to undo his vest, smoothed his chest with his hand, scratched his side and raised his head again:

"That weakling was the only one who fought back – the only one! And you remember in training – I bet there were others who saw that bastard Zhusipbekov going through pockets, but only Raskolnikov spoke out. You remember training, don't you?"

"I remember," I said. "I remember it well. Go on with you, time to sleep. Everything is fine. The bad times are over. We've made it – like real men... and that's all there is to it."

Serioga grunted but then smiled at me and said:

"The mare was pitied by the wolf which spared her tail and hoof."

And he walked away, waving his belt wrapped round his right hand, slapped a recruit, who was coming back from cleaning the toilet, laughed in a false, shaky voice, and said out loud to the whole barracks:

"I'm a middler and I still can't believe I don't owe anyone anything."

And there was a sound like a convulsive sob. Thank God everyone was asleep. Just one terrified rookie raised his head.

Serioga must have overdone the spirit after all.

A series of ideas came into my head, simple and grey as fence boards, one after the other; I'd been through a lot – at least a third of my time – and everything I'd experienced would be unchanged forever. I'll never forget it and it'll be my life. Nothing else will ever grow in that place. Only this and only so. Interesting, strange, and frightening.

Serioga went on leave.

Raskolnikov's arm healed in two weeks. They went to beat him up a couple of times, I think, but it didn't work out – something got in the way and they just threatened him through the window. He was sent straight from the hospital to another unit. Apparently, there wasn't any intimidation there, but the whole detachment had to run cross country round the barracks for the slightest fault. It was heaven for rookies and a prison camp for the middlers and the dads – everything the other way round, but actually the same.

For some reason I wanted to see Raskolnikov and say good-bye but I didn't have the chance – they took him off quietly, before breakfast. It was strange, I'd never spoken to him, except that one night in the toilet when we were rookies, the first night, but I always had the impression he was thinking about me all the time and knew that I was thinking about him. We'd seen the last of each other, I thought – over and done. And thank God for it. But I was wrong again.

He came back to us in the summer. I forget when exactly, some time at the end of July or start of August. That was the worst of the low times – all the dads are down and bored. There's nothing inside you except that you want to go home. It isn't missing your flat or your friends, girls or your cassette machine. You miss another life, and you don't quite know whether it's a longing for something else or the hate for your present existence you're so sick of. It's a time when every dad goes crazy in his own way.

Korovin went on benders and got drunk – they called him by his name and patronymic in the cooler and kept a special bunk for him. Near the end of his service Igor Petrenko got bad news from his girlfriend – there was some problem between them and he was either in a foul mood, like a new middler who has just been through all the pain, or sleeping all hours of the day. I threw myself into what remained of my service, got a junior sergeant's rank, and they put me in charge of a squad. My shift had the best results on combat duty. I passed with first class on Aviation Day. I tried my best, did everything I could to be allowed home first, in the envied zero batch for demob. That was hard: there were only three places in the zero batch, and one of them was reserved for the unit commander's driver. I read political information too. The political officer even thought I might be some use and started conversations on sensitive topics when there was no one else in the barracks, but I turned him down with a smile – better not to get involved in that sort of thing.

While my shift slept ahead of a night duty, I went to the Lenin room apparently to go through newspapers but in fact to stare out at the pavement where Natasha, the pretty wife of the bespectacled major, went to work and back. I had cooled down a bit, and didn't bother waiting for her on the street but I still looked – her walk and her strong body had a promise of something to come.

Somebody lives with women like that, makes love to them… If only it was me.

Serioga Barintsov was calmer than most, he had gone lazy, rosy-cheeked and put on weight – back to his old self. He was just like a tom cat playing whatever game he felt like: suddenly turning on the rookies, screwing his face into tragic expressions, giving the middlers a hard time by accusing them of imaginary faults and omissions, going to see films, visiting the nurses' hostel with Korovin, after which he told me such stories that I laughed all evening till I cried. We had long talks in the evening. I invited the rookie Vasya Smagin to come down from the top bunks. His nickname was "the correspondent" – he worked as a clerk and wrote about our unit in the regional paper, so he knew lots of interesting things.

Some time in July or August Barintsov told me they'd brought Raskolnikov back. I was just getting up from a sleep ahead of night duty. I put a towel round my neck and went to the camp office, and there was Raskolnikov standing sadly by the wall, white-faced with a fresh black eye and his kit bag over his shoulders. He just squinted at me. Petrenko stood opposite, bristling his imposing moustache and asking in a soft and cajoling voice:

"So Raskolnikov…was it better there?"

Vasya Smagin, who spent time buzzing around the office, told me exactly what had happened to Raskolnikov. He'd caught a lung complaint and they sent him for a month to Tambov – for a whole month. I don't know if he'd really needed that much time to get better, or whether the head doctor had agreed to let him hang around. When he was leaving they told him he'd go back via Moscow, undergo tests there and send the results back to Tambov where they'd decide whether he was fit or not – maybe he'd need to come back for more treatment. He did the tests in Moscow and the results would only be ready the next day. So he decided to wait, probably hoping that he could get back into hospital. But his leave-of-absence papers were already overdue and instead of staying at home he stood like a sore thumb all night in Paveletsky Station. A patrol noticed him and took him in. They kept him 24 hours at the Aleshkinsky Barracks and then sent him back to his unit. Raskolnikov's offence ruined a whole year's good performance results for the unit, which was sent on a route march with full equipment. Raskolnikov's senior comrades-in-arms gave him a black eye for his troubles and to remember them by, and the commanders got rid of their black sheep by sending him back to us.

We went to the cafeteria to sit for a while after lunch. A delegation of middlers – Lang, Djikia, Vashakidze and Korobchik – came over to Petrenko.

"Igor," Lang said cautiously, "let Raskolnikov do his time. He sneaked on us, like a rat. He turned us in. He's always looking for cushy numbers – let him do his time now, so he knows what it's really like in the army."

"Well, what's it to me..." Petrenko said simply. "Let him – so long as it doesn't spoil my demob."

Igor was very concerned about his demob – he wanted to be in the zero batch too, and wanted to be a sergeant-major by the time he quit.

"What's the matter with you, Oleg," he asked me, frowning unpleasantly. "You don't like it? But it's true – he never wanted to do his time. He always wanted to get out of it, didn't he? And the middlers will come down on him anyway, whatever I say ᴛᴏ them…"

"Come on, you rascals, let's have another Pepsi," Serioga Barinstev said to relieve the tension. "God rest the soul of lance-corporal Raskolnikov."

I soon calmed down. They didn't hit Raskolnikov much. The middlers worked out a more cunning plan – they let the rookies use Raskolnikov. They told them – "Go ask Raskolnikov to clean the toilets. If he won't, you'll have to go do it yourself." It was wickedly funny to see the frightened, harassed rookie, Kuritsyn, sidle up to Raskolnikov and mutter: "In the toilet… can you give us a hand, a bit of help…" Raskolnikov would go red, try to turn away and do something else – dig around in his cupboard under the severe looks of the middlers, mutter that he already helped once today and couldn't do it right now. Then Kuritsyn would whine: "Come on, help," and there'd be some hissing comments from the middlers, and Raskolnikov would put his head down and go, and Kuritsyn, putting his head down even more, went behind him, looking from side to side as if to ask: Is this OK, are the middlers and dads still playing the game?

It was a real show. And the rookies gradually became bolder. I even heard that one of them hit our lance-corporal while the dads pretended not to notice.

There were a lot of funny stories about Raskolnikov. One time the sergeant told Raskolnikov to sleep on Vashakidze's bed – Raskolnikov never seemed to be able to find a free place to sleep. That night Korobchik, who teased and was friends with our quartermaster-sergeant Vashakidze, came back from a trip and went straight to his bed to wake him. Raskolnikov always slept with his head covered, curled up on his side as if he was trying to disappear into the bed.

Korobchik sat down gently on the edge of the bed, but Raskolnikov must have woken up straight away and been ready for trouble, whether it was work, a beating or just a harmless joke by some dad who couldn't sleep. Korobchik took careful aim with fingers and grabbed the sleeper – Vashakidze, as he thought – by the nose. Raskolnikov must have thought his time had come. He sprang up like a scalded cat, yelped, and jumped into the middle of the dorm, still holding his blanket. Korobchik was mortified, he even seemed a little ashamed of himself.

Serioga and I had a desultory laugh when we saw this. We couldn't sleep and Vasya Smagin was telling us about American presidents.

Vasya was an interesting boy. He always had a pleasant smile, never said no if a dad asked him to put a heartfelt and well-written message on a postcard or make up a letter to a girl with plenty of love and regret. He found a way of smoothing every dad – he would ask them about home, about what they did before the army or about their love life, and he was such a good listener you couldn't believe it wasn't what interested Vasya more than anything else in the world just then. I tried to do the same but I found it too hard to pretend – I disliked the part too much while to Vasya it came naturally. The dads looked after him a bit and if he had trouble it was on the quiet from resentful middlers. I didn't know how it would go for him when our generation demobbed – would they forgive him?

The most striking thing about Vasya was his curiosity about how people had been as rookies, who had got beaten the worst, who had tried to ingratiate himself, how dads break people, who had been friends with whom, what people had been like as middlers, and what sort of rookie makes a respected dad, and what exactly that is. I wondered to myself after he'd finished asking his questions. What did he think when he found out that Petrenko, Barintsov, Raskolnikov and me had been in the same platoon in training? What did he think when he heard that? He'd been even more thoughtful than usual when he asked about that. But I couldn't think of anything.

When Vasya saw the scene in the middle of the night between Raskolnikov and Korobchik he suddenly said:

"What a terrible fate…"

"You mean Raskolnikov?" I asked.

"Yes."

"Why?" Barintsov asked in an empty voice, and pulled his blanket higher. His face was in shadow.

"The boy sneaked on his mates. Now the boy is paying for it," I sighed. I always had a feeling when I spoke to Vasya that someone else was speaking instead of me.

"He's not so poor, no poorer than anyone else," Barintsov added from the darkness.

Vasya agreed quickly and readily, nodded and went on telling us about how John Kennedy was killed. He was good at forgetting his words and changing the subject, so it was often hard to work out what he was driving at. Later I saw out of the corner of my eye how Vasya went up to Raskolnikov and asked him a short question and studied our lance-corporal with unnatural interest without coming too close to him, as if knowing that the person he was talking to had a fatal illness. Vasya was a lot like me, and that drew me to him.

Life was dull but quiet.

But then, after the demob order was issued everyone erupted. The veterans couldn't wait to go home, there were rumours going round about who'd be demobbed in what order and how they'd fixed it: that so and so sneaked to the political officer, someone else had busted a gut to impress the sergeant-major. They talked about what obligatory task each of us would have to do before we were allowed home – what you needed to do to get sent home before the snow, which was what they used to frighten layabouts. Those who were going later got to hate those who were going earlier. There hadn't been much by way of friendship before, but now people looked daggers at each other. That made everything even worse.

Ten days after the demob order the camp commander told us all at parade that there would be three people in the zero batch: his driver, sergeant Petrenko and junior sergeant Maltsev – me. I relaxed: that was it, all over. I spent the evenings getting my parade uniform ready. I started to think when I would say good-bye to gorgeous Natasha, the major's wife. The rookie's passion had completely gone, but I still wanted to give her flowers and say those words.

Barintsov laughed at me.

"I told you – who needs flowers?! Just a bottle and straight to her flat – forward into battle. What does she get from flowers? Do you know what she wants? Maybe she'd like it more with a common soldier. Something different, ha ha…"

But I wanted to do it my way. I told Vasya Smagin about my plan. I don't know what he thought – he just smiled and said nothing.

My head was sometimes so full of ideas it felt ready to burst: I'd go back to college, see my friends, meet girls… yes, girls – find me the prettiest and most enigmatic, with long wavy hair, and don't turn the others away either. I'll be powerful and brave, a real man! Life would be straightforward and clear, from top to bottom.

It's hard to explain.

Even I find it hard to understand now. I regret that feeling of lightness and complete freedom, when you feel like saying: I don't care how I am dressed, what people say when I go past, what I'll eat and whether I'll eat at all, how much money I have and what's around me – I don't care! All that matters is that I go where I want to go. I sleep as much as I want to sleep. I don't give a damn about any of you, about anyone or everyone.

The veterans were at fever pitch and it ended badly.

A week before the zero batch was due home, four veterans who'd sent a rookie for vodka were caught and told they'd serve till the snow came. One of the four was Serioga Barintsov – he went black in the face and started to sleep face down. Someone had told tales about the vodka. And there wasn't a moment's doubt who'd done it. At night Petrenko and two of the veterans hooded Raskolnikov and beat him up. He didn't try to resist when they wrapped him in a blanket and dragged him down the aisle with his legs flailing, and the only sound in the dorm was a muffled howling, an animal sound. Petrenko didn't make much effort to hide his identity. He said loudly: "Don't even dream of hanging yourself, you turd. None of us want to be sent to penal battalion for your rotten sake. You can sneak all you want, you bastard!"

Raskolnikov was immediately put in hospital – he had some bad injuries and a slight concussion. The camp commanders explained it as a fall down stairs. Petrenko expected his zero batch to be cancelled any minute, but there wasn't a sound. Either Raskolnikov had kept quiet or the commanders understood that if they touched anyone, it would be curtains for Raskolnikov.

I felt sorry for Serioga Barintsov – he wilted completely and lay for hours, apparently calm, looking straight up in the air, as if waiting for his time to come.

"Never mind," he said, "we'll get home anyhow."

The zero batch was leaving early on Monday morning. On Friday I bought twenty-one tulips from an old lady at the garrison and I was there waiting for Natasha at the checkpoint.

She came alone, which was what I wanted, what I'd dreamt of for a year and a half. She looked over people's heads, her lips sealed haughtily, seeming to float over everyone or through everyone with her set, proud expression, as if carried along by the wind. She walked, putting her irresistible legs through the slits in her coat. She came nearer and alongside me. I forced myself forward.

"Excuse me," I said tensely.

Everyone at the checkpoint stared at my back. She didn't understand at first that she'd been addressed and she went past a little way but then frowned and glanced at me as if to ask "Are you talking to me?"

"Excuse me," I repeated without a pause. "I am holding you up, excuse me…"

She had a polite calm face, which I couldn't bring myself to look at, she smelt of perfume while I was at the end of my army service with sweaty palms grasping those flowers and trying to find a way of expressing all the pain and the emotion…

"Here, take these, please. And thank you." I tried to hand her the bouquet.

"What? Who are they from? Who told you? You can tell him…" She took an angry breath and furrowed her plucked eyebrows over the bridge of her nose.

"No! These are only from me. And from all of us. I want… Thank you!"

"From you? But thank you for what? What are you so nervous about?"

She looked at the bouquet as if it were a dirty kitten and I felt as if I was falling into her, straight into her beautiful face, into the incredible turn of her head and the voice, which spoke like someone who had once belonged to me.

"They are for your beauty," I blurted out. "Take them please. Don't upset me," I said so pitifully that I felt ashamed of myself, and I thrust the bouquet towards her.

"All right, all right," she said quickly. "I'll take them. Let's do this. We'll give the flowers to these lads at the checkpoint, and they can put them here in the window. So that everyone who goes by will be able to enjoy them. Like that… isn't that nice?"

"Yes, OK," I nodded, trembling as I felt the touch of her body in the soft movement with which she took the bouquet.

She passed the bouquet into the hands of the moustachioed warrant officer, who barely stifled a guffaw while the duty soldiers behind the window were groaning out loud with laughter.

A dark-haired, well-groomed senior lieutenant, adjutant of the general at the college, put his head out of a black Volga:

"Natasha, are we off?"

He dismissed the driver with a majestic wave and came over to us.

"Flowers, eh? From who?"

"From him." Natasha waved her white arm, like a swan's neck, towards me. "That boy... he says it's for being beautiful," and she gave a quick smile.

I raised my face – she had crow's feet around her eyes.

"Pri-ivate soldier," the adjutant said in a drawl, raising his eyebrows mockingly. "From you, eh? You must've been saving up for a month? More like six months! Right? Who do you think you are? Be off with you. What did you save on? Collars, maybe... your collar's a bit on the dirty side. Maybe we haven't been washing our neck, am I right?"

Natasha suddenly threw her head back and giggled in a false, shrill voice:

"Leave the boy alone – he'll wash his neck!"

"Off you go," the senior lieutenant dismissed me.

He turned away, but I stood there, I couldn't put one foot in front of the other.

The lieutenant saw an opportunity for more laughs. He hissed at me:

"Comrade soldier: have you forgotten how to walk? Do you need teaching?"

I smiled straight into his well-groomed face. My God, this is it!

"You could try!"

The jaws of the duty soldiers at the checkpoint dropped open.

"Wha-at!" the lieutenant bawled. "Which unit?" I named a random five figures, and the lieutenant wrote them straight down in a notebook and shouted some more: "I'll spoil your mood, boy, get out of here, quick march!" And he gave my shoulder a shove.

He shouldn't have done that.

I stepped back and landed a pleasurable punch on his handsome swarthy face, on the electric bell at six in the morning, on the lonely lump of lard in mashed potato, on the puttees with blue streaks, on ugly faces and my mother's voice from the white envelope, on my past life and the trampled twenty-one tulips, which will be taken by the prostitutes, who creep up to the checkpoint after midnight, on myself and the person I would never be again.

The lieutenant gave a cry, staggered, and reached trembling for his cap – the expression on his face was ridiculous. Natasha stood frozen with a disgusted grimace, which made her face ugly and unrecognisable. I ran off along the fence. I had to get across the fence where they wouldn't see me and get to roll call – I was on duty for the last time.

After roll call I told everything to Serioga.

"Rubbish," he said at once. "They won't find you. What have you got to worry about – they haven't the time to find you, you've only got two more days. Just don't blab – you should have taken me to the toilet and told me there instead of standing in the middle of the barracks. Anyway, good boy, you met your love. Just two days."

I did a lot of funny things during the shift: asked the new middlers to forgive me, made Vasya Smagin a present of my badges, carried Kuritsyn on my back to the toilet. I was in a fever, so I cooled it by walking in the wet autumn forest, staring at the firs and maples, and the remnants of blue sky amid the ragged clouds, like lumps of poplar down.

"Maltsev," the telephone orderly called me from the porch. I stepped behind him into the commander's office. The commander was sitting behind a desk in a greatcoat with the political officer; on the left there was a sergeant-major and my adjutant with a strained expression.

"That's him," the adjutant said. "Thanks for finding him. God job!"

"So we're decided," said the commander, as if I wasn't there. "He gets his things together, health check and five days in the cooler, and then we'll see. Is that all right?"

The sergeant major looked me straight in the eyes and said a whistling whisper:

"You'll see your mum when it snows."

Back in barracks I hugged Petrenko – he was off tomorrow, so I wouldn't see him again. I nodded to Barintsov – he'd still be there.

Serioga said to me severely:

"We'll find that bastard. The sneak will be sorry he was ever born."

In the hospital Sergei the orderly checked my blood pressure and when the nurse went out he asked:

"D'you want us to get you off the cooler?"

"No."

"Why do you look green?" the nurse asked jokily. "Don't go yet, sit on the bench in the corridor, I'll bring you some vitamins at least. You hooligan, you."

The sergeant who'd brought me chatted with the nurse about some girl called Allochka. I went out of the room, and walked towards the window – I wanted to look down from the fourth floor. The window was open, Raskolnikov was standing on the windowsill in blue pyjamas filling cracks with plaster – winter was coming on. He wore a strange expression, it had a sort of tranquillity under the blue sky. I went towards him slowly and when I reached him, I grabbed him by both legs and, thrusting with my shoulder, I started to push his quivering body onto the shaky tin of the outside sill.

"What are you doing?" He didn't shout, he moaned.

The jar of plaster shattered into pieces down below and then the screwdriver fell as his hands clutched at me.

"Tell me, you swine, or I'll kill you! Is it you who sneaked?! Is it you who tells on us, you? Tell me or I'll kill you!" I spoke calmly, my voice was hollow.

"Well!!!" I pulled him as hard as I could, and he cried: "It's me! Me!"

I stopped still, my hands relaxed and he collapsed on the floor. He couldn't stand, his knees were trembling, he wrapped his hands around them and hid his terrified face.

"Here are your vitamins, soldier," the nurse called from the ward.

I came back from the cooler as calm as ice. I knew I had nothing to look forward to now.

Serioga was on duty and while I was waiting for him I washed my shirt which was black after work in the cooler, handed in the parade uniform, which I'd prepared for demob, at the quartermaster's stores. Somebody had unscrewed the emblems and pulled the plastic stripes out of the epaulettes, but what did it matter.

The shift jumped out of the lorry, Korobchik sent one of the rookies for hot water. I stood by the porch and they all gathered round me.

"Where's Barintsov?" I asked Smagin who was pulling some banner off the back of the lorry.

"Barintsov has demobbed," Smagin smiled at me cautiously. "He went in the zero batch."

I turned and took a few steps to one side along the black asphalt. Smagin added insistently:

"Do you remember, he was the first middler to get leave as well, for some reason."

He was waiting to see my expression when I turned to look at him. He was surprised to see me smiling. Well… what's the difference.

For a month and a half I did kitchen duty every other day with the fresh recruits and rookies. My last kitchen shift was at the end of November, a day before demob.

"Oleg, you're wanted out there," said the rookie Shvyrin and nodded in an indefinite direction.

I wiped my hands on the greasy apron and went out into the raw November expanse.

It was Raskolnikov in parade uniform with his suitcase.

"It's me," he said.

I nodded – I could see it was him.

"I wanted to say, that…"

"I know," I said huskily, "I've got it now."

There is no blue in the November sky – it is like snow after a housewife has beaten her carpet on it.

"Well, what are you standing there for?" I asked him.

He turned and went.

The political deputy called me in when I had my documents and could go.

"Well, Maltsev, what are you plans after demob? College? Do you still remember maths? What are you going to get stuck in?"

"Life," I shrugged.

"Listen, Maltsev," the deputy said bluntly. "Don't go and see Barintsov. You'd beat him up or he'd beat you up – what's the point?"

"Yes," I said. "Sure."

I was home in three days. The sky was sinking to evening, darkening like fresh asphalt. My mother made my bed and cried as she turned on the water in the bath. My father sat with his big hands on the table and looked at the neck of the bottle. That was all.

"Lena Zvonareva has grown up so. You won't recognize her," my mother said, bringing cushions into the room. "Such a girl she's become…"

"What are you going to do now? Straight to college? Or go somewhere for a holiday? Or go visit a friend. When I demobbed in 1954, Egypt was just starting…"

"Straight to college."

I went out in the yard for a breath of fresh air. It had got much colder. Two girls went by and burst out laughing in the stair porch. They whispered: "Maltsev is back".

I am Maltsev.

I went to bed – like diving into a well.

I woke at six o'clock, looked at the ceiling, got up, got a glass of water and went to the window.

My mother was looking at my back. She'd waited for me at that window.

The sky was bending, as if exhausted, over the mud and the black, shivering branches. The first snow started to fall, hardly noticeable at first, then thicker, circling and twirling – light, fluffy, melting as it met the ground, like a ghostly mesh covering everything, like slanting, soft locks of hair on someone you love, fluttering in the wind. It was snowing.

I stood, looked at the snow and turned back to sleep some more.

THE FOOL

From the stories
of lance-corporal Smagin

This was the first time I'd been in the unit's hospital, so I was in a state of suspicious withdrawal – I wanted to be sure from the outset of avoiding any blunders and mistakes, which could make me dependent on anyone. In the army that state of mind is exaggerated and never goes away. The army teaches you to value independence.

I took an immediate dislike to the man in the next bed. He was specially concerned about my arrival and gave me all manner of advice – orders, in fact:

"Lie down here, here – understand? You have the top part of the bedside table. How long have you been in the army? Still a rookie, then… Go and get your linen, right?! Leave your bag… What are you doing standing there?"

I followed his ramblings at first, but then decided they'd only get worse and were best put a stop to sooner rather than later, so I jumped right out of the regime he was proposing: chucked my wash bag and crumpled paperback on the bed, wandered over to the window, leant my palms on the sill and looked down at the dirty snow outside, where a child with a spade was relentlessly pursuing a clumsy crow.

The sight of my unconcerned back irritated him.

"Go on, go on! What're you waiting for? The nurse who gives out linen will finish work and then what'll you do? It's mealtime soon. The head doctor will see on his rounds that you've no pyjamas and send you back to your unit in no time. D'you hear?"

In a minute he'll be telling me I'm undermining the country's defence potential by just standing here, I thought to myself with a shiver.

"D'you hear me? Are you deaf? Eh?"

He jerked himself off the bed, swore, pulled on an errant slipper and came over to me.

"What can you see out there?"

He looked down, then fidgeted to try and see the view from exactly where I stood, and finally recited into my ear:

"Don't you hear what I'm saying? What are you standing there for? Do as I tell you. D'you hear? What're you waiting for? Go on." He shouted the last words.

I turned and looked straight at him sternly. It was a tried-and-tested way of confounding fools, which was certainly what my neighbour was.

He was small and skinny, with sunken cheeks on a spotty face and a bent trampoline of a nose. The blue eyes under his eyebrows, which were pulled together over his nose, looked at me with questioning surprise. He swept his hair the colour of dried reeds over to one side and organized the white trench of his parting.

"What's the matter?" He swore, sizing me up. "Funny in the head? D'you want waking at half past one in the morning?"

"You could try," I said to myself, keeping a steady, intense gaze fixed on him, waiting for him to twig that what I meant to convey was puzzlement. Puzzlement and contempt.

"Nothing to say? Idiot... Stands and says nothing." He squeezed out a laugh. "Go on, stand then, stand..." He pretended to laugh again, and hissed as he turned away: "Rookie!"

"That's it, he's finished," I thought to myself. "I should have hit him. One punch... I could have..."

He went out. He didn't slam the door but slipped through it nervously.

I stirred from where I was, came over to the bed, sat down, held my head in my fists and listened to my heart beating and the clicking metal cricket of the clock. I sat there, my nose wheezing, and thought tiredly: "I must be a nut... I'm a nut... it's probably true... An unhealthy, exaggerated sense of sovereignty... Rubbish, I'm talking rubbish... Just a nut." And I listened to the dull beating of my heart deep inside my body.

I wandered up and down the ward all day, mesmerized

by the idleness, silence and peace. An express train will sometimes brake on a straight run across country, losing speed so that birdsong and the tender rustling of leaves start to penetrate the shocked scraping of the wheels as the brakes grasp them. That scraping is a reminder of the speed that burnt your soul – an insubstantial, worthless memory – and it was personified by my fellow patient, Shurik Shapovalenko, soldier of the second platoon in our company, the guard platoon, which manned checkpoints round the camp.

Shurik frowned and went silent every time I came into the ward. When I spoke he tensed up, twitched the corners of his thin lips and snorted gently, expressing profound contempt for my impossibly stupid and pointless words. He told all the other patients that I was a pen pusher, took no part in active service, and never left the camp office. I took a casual view and I wasn't even angry when I caught him reading my army passport, which he had found in my bedside table. "Jour-nal-ist," he read my pre-army profession and threw the passport on the bed with a nasty, contemptuous laugh.

I wasn't angry. The soul of a man in the army, in a brutal company of men, who don't pardon weakness and have little use for compassion and kindness, is full of tension. That tension was now unwinding with every blessed, intoxicating hour of idleness. Shurik's encroachments were nothing at all compared with the ocean of freedom and rest, which I was drinking down in gulps.

My train was braking.

I went to bed at half past nine, not bothering with the scheduled film.

"Hey, journalist, rise and shine! Time to get up, Mr Correspondent!" It was Shurik shaking me by the shoulder.

It was clear from his voice that he meant to balance on the edge of a joke: either he was afraid of going too far or the film had put him in good spirits.

I didn't feel like joking. I sat up in bed, looked hard at the clock, saw that it was midnight and, without looking at him, lay down with my face to the wall.

"Time to get up, time to get up! Hey, Mr Correspondent, time to get up," he said in a nasal voice, trying to roll me out of bed, like a log that had got jammed. I kept quiet and paid no attention to his efforts. Then he took me by both shoulders and tried to pull me up, increasingly irritated by the lack of reaction. Then he bent down and shouted in my ear, touching it lightly with his lips:

"Time to get up! Mr Correspondent, up! Let's get up!"

I didn't open an eye. He sat on me and started bouncing up and down.

"As much as you like," I thought.

He had done half a year more than me, so he was allowed to do this and I was supposed to submit. But my train had braked – I showed complete contempt for this "middler".

"Maybe you've died," he giggled, put out his hand and slapped me across the face with the palm of his hand.

It was a light slap, the usual sort. That's how they hit you normally. Either in the stomach or with the palm of the hand in the face. So there are no marks afterwards. It works – there aren't any marks.

He slapped me lightly, playfully even.

I was tired of the grinding sound of the train. I wanted to hear the forest and the birds, even for a short while.

I sat up in bed. Shurik stood beside me, smiling in the darkness.

I rubbed my eyes, turned back the blanket, freed my legs, felt for my slippers, pushed my shirt into by pants, stood up, and even before I was standing straight I grabbed Shurik by the collar and jerked him towards me. I squeezed his throat with no idea what I was doing and why.

He shouted with surprise and anger:

"What're you doing, journalist?!" and pulled at my hands with his claws, trying weakly to loosen them. "What are you…?" He croaked and jerked his head, instead of hitting me in the face. If he'd done that I'd have thrown him back on the bed and hit him with my fist from the right as he got up. And again and again! But it didn't occur to him to strike instead of trying vainly to weaken my grip.

I pushed him away, shook my slippers off my feet and sat down, exhaling the stifling, mad air from my lungs.

"Nutter… But you did get up… I made you get up," Shurik whined, breathing heavily.

"That's it. He won't hit me now. So that's it." I figured and lay down, pulling the covers over my head.

Shurik settled down too, muttering in a thin voice. When he was in bed, he went quiet and said, putting his hands behind his head:

"Journalist, why don't you write a book about me, eh? Eh?" he quacked. "I know I give you a hard time…"

I smiled wryly: Shurik obviously didn't know what a hard time good people – equal people – can give each other. His efforts were comical and petty, and one even felt sorry for him in a disgusted sort of way.

"Write about me!"

"Books get written about people, who are interesting to everyone else," I stated the truism.

"Why is my life not interesting? Everyone wants to read about the life of an ordinary person."

"Your life wouldn't be of interest to anybody," I said and then sugared the pill, "like most people's lives. At best your grandchildren will remember you, but your great grandchildren will forget you. In a hundred years time nobody will remember about you, and you will never be remembered again. In a few billion years the sun will burn up the earth… and nobody will remember anybody – everybody and everything will be dust… from Lenin to the pharaohs… So who'd be bothered about you – a speck of dust in this life?" I wanted his wretched little soul to feel the chill of eternity.

Like mine did.

"A speck of dust... My life? What do you know about my life, journalist?" he said, puffing himself up. He thought for a moment what else to say, made a gurgling sound in his throat and turned to the wall.

I drifted into sleep with a feeling I'd had before: a feeling of something weighing heavy, pressing unbearably on my heart.

It happens when you hear somebody else's confession – you look into another person's soul without wanting to. It's like getting dirt on a clean, white sheet. Nothing tangible has happened, but it's as if rust has settled weightlessly and immovably on your soul and you don't know how to chase the feeling away.

Shurik was discharged in the morning. I didn't know about it. I just noticed his stooped figure with head lowered from behind, at a distance. He spent a while adjusting his coat in front of the mirror, then stood for a bit and finally stepped towards the door. Shurik slowed down when he reached the door, looked around quickly with his sharp-nosed pale face, and the door slammed shut. That was it.

He had gone and his bed was made, as if no one had slept there. And time would blow him out of mind with an indifferent gust. It already had.

The reason I didn't know he had been discharged is that I went early in the morning for electrophoresis treatment. "Go now," the hospital orderly, lance-corporal Klygin told me in a secretive whisper, "there's a young nurse…" And he smiled, pursing his lips in the shape of a bucket handle.

The lance-corporal was tall and stately, with a golden crop of hair and a ruddy complexion. The whole garrison knew him and the whole garrison liked him for his endless jokes and occasional kindnesses, when he provided safe haven in the hospital to friends, who were having a tough time in the unit and needed to sit it out and wait until things died down. But the orderly's kindness was only available to a chosen few. People referred to him with envy and respect when they saw the broad-shouldered figure in a well-ironed coat stepping into the mess to fetch rations for the hospital.

He had a good life. He only spent the nights in the barracks and he got up to any tricks he pleased in the hospital: playing hide and seek, tig or blind man's buff with the patients, and laughing so loud that guards at the checkpoint looked round and smiled in the direction of the hospital. He even used to chase a patient out of bed and take a nap after lunch. That's what you call living well. Service in the medical corps was a doddle. That's what was said in the garrison. One of the favourite topics for soldiers is who has it easy in the army. The stories get generously peppered with invention and all sorts of fantastic tales are made up. Envy is blind and doesn't like plain prose: maybe life wasn't really as good as all that for lance-corporal Klygin, but the general opinion was unshakeable.

What's more, he was doing his army stint in his home town. God only knows how he'd managed to arrange that. But to be at home was excellent in itself. Girls of his acquaintance from "outside" often came to see him. Their disturbing, excited laughter could be heard from the orderly's room, which was locked from inside, and afterwards they floated like visions past the patients who stiffened in their beds. Klygin, like any male celebrity, was reckoned to be an uncommon specialist in all matters amorous, so if he said that now was the time to go for electrophoresis, now was the time.

I knocked a couple of times on the door, which had a plate with the number I'd been told, and went in, my slippers shuffling over the linoleum. The room was filled with a chaotic array of flowers in tubs and pots, brought here from other rooms, which were being redecorated. I picked up an hourglass and turned it over. The sand began to run through.

The door let someone in and the sheet of paper with my treatment instructions was snatched from my hands before I had time to bring them from behind my back. A girl in a white coat went over to the table and looked at the instructions. I glanced quickly at her short dark hair, full red lips and eye make-up, and immediately looked down at her white boots and the jeans that were tucked into them. They were good quality jeans.

"Come here," she said, with female precision, lightly touching my shaky hand.

I bent my head even lower and stepped towards the cabin she indicated, intensely aware of my woodenness. I hadn't been in the army long but I'd completely forgotten how to look girls straight in the face. Somehow I was reminded of a savage clutching a crystal vase – a pretty thing but a club is more to the point.

I lay down on the couch, embarrassed by my grey underwear, and peered at the ceiling; the girl put a strip of metal on my chest in business-like fashion, pressed it down with a little bag and made a clicking noise with something.

"Now you will feel a prickling sensation. Like a mustard plaster. A good mustard plaster, not an old one," she explained.

"It's too strong – weaker would be better," I said faintly.

"Now, now, don't be weak," she said in a matter-of-fact way, turned something on the control panel and disappeared behind a screen, leaving me in a cloud of scent, which played havoc with my imagination.

"I'm not weak. I've been spoilt," I started a conversation with myself. "What's the difference? If you're weak you take any situation in life as it comes, but if you've been spoilt you want to ensure maximum comfort in any situation. Being spoilt is better than being weak – it means you're more enterprising." I talked to myself, like everyone in the army does. When you can't answer out loud you answer to yourself. It gives an illusion of equality. If you can't be a human being out loud, you try to be a human being to yourself.

"Wake up! What are you, funny in the head?"

Heck, I'd drifted off. And of course the wake-up call had me leaping up, as it does all of us in the army. The reflex gets instilled. Everything on my chest scattered to the floor and I was frantically feeling for the bedside table with my shirt in it.

She stood and held back laughter as she watched me resentfully pull on my underwear and pyjamas and quickly smooth the sheet on the couch. I said, "thank you" as I went out, and caught sight in the mirror of a couple of tomatoes, which had once been my ears.

"Well, Correspondent, what do you make of our Allochka?" Klygin asked with a smile.

He liked to talk and I was a good listener and good at nodding understandingly in agreement, so he enjoyed chatting at me.

"Yeah," I said bashfully, playing the role I usually played with Klygin, the one that worked best for me, of a provincial simpleton, who brings out people's protective instinct.

"Too right," he went on with enthusiasm. "She's straight out of medical college. Like a colour TV – you can't take your eyes off her. It certainly goes on in medical college… even though she walks about looking as if you wouldn't stand a chance. Hmmm. I'd have tried it on ages ago. But her father is the chief doctor in the garrison.

I rounded my eyes in surprise and said timidly: "Yeah?"

"That's right," Klygin went on in full flow. "I bet the correspondent has got his eye on her. But I pass on that one. Taboo. Hmmm."

After lunch I had a forest of cupping glasses attached to my back and lay in bed on my stomach, struggling to stay awake and listening to the chatter of junior sergeant Vanya Tsvetkov, who was second-in-command of the commandant's platoon. Tsvetkov was talking a lot of nonsense.

"Shurik Shapovalenko was in here before you — a middler from our platoon. Did you see him? What d'you make of him? Bit strange? That's nothing. He's a fool, a total wally. He has the whole company in stitches. They've given him a nickname — the lance-corporal. When he was on the third checkpoint, Lang decided to play a trick on him for a laugh: 'Shurik,' he said, 'they're making you lance-corporal, the lads at the switchboard heard the company commander talking about it.' The fool was dead pleased and ran off to see Vashakidze in the stores. He got some stripes and stuck them on when he was on duty that night. He turned up the next morning in the mess with the stripes on. Petrenko stopped him — he's one of the main dads in our lot. What d'you think you're doing, you scabby middler, he says — are you off your head? And he tore off the stripes on both sides. Right off. Petrenko's a tough guy, a miner.

And Shurik, the wet dummy, stood there looking at him, blinking and twitching his lips. The wally. The whole mess was in an uproar. Breakfast was delayed fifteen minutes."

I took care to smile at the bits the teller found amusing. Tsvetkov was easily carried away, so I had to smile every couple of sentences.

I could be sleeping now. The thought came to me every time I smiled.

Tsvetkov had now got into a well-worn rut and our conversation (or rather his monologue) was stuck in it.

"And then he fell in love. Why do I always put him on the third checkpoint? Because Allochka goes to work that way. You saw the bint in the test room? Well he fancies her – how about that? She sometimes says a couple of words to him or gives him a smile when she goes past… And he puffs himself up, all important… That's why he dreamt of getting promoted to lance corporal… And he was pestering Vashakidze for her photos. When they issue passes you have to supply two photos, one for the pass and the other goes to records, where Vashakidze is in charge. So Vashakidze said ito him, 'OK, but you'll have to bring me some treats from the canteen.' Maybe he was just messing about. But, sure enough, after lunch Shurik brought treats." Tsvetkov caught his breath merrily and made round eyes. "Two bottles of Pepsi, a bottle of Fanta, five meat pies and some cream cones – a real feast. After that he had to use worn-out inside collars – he hadn't any money for new ones. So I put him on a few extra details for that… What a wally."

I gave him a nice big understanding smile. I could be fast asleep.

"The whole company knows that Shurik's in love and who with. As soon as he gets back from duty Barintsov or Korovin call him over, sit him down and ask, 'So, Shipa,' (that's what we call him), 'how's Allochka?' He goes red, doesn't say anything and just wipes his face. The dads are falling about – what a fool! Her house is the one across the road from the garrison, and her windows look out on the third checkpoint. Shipa is always gazing up at her windows – does he expect her to start undressing or what? Wally! He may spy her in the window maybe only once an evening, but Shipa will spend all night out in the freezing cold, he'll freeze solid and the other guard can sit nice and warm inside. There's no shortage of volunteers to do a shift with Shipa, and spend all the time in the warmth. Vashakidze and Lang told him for a joke, 'Allochka asked on the way back from work if you could drop by to see her about some books'." Tsvetkov's eyes glistened like two lumps of ice in the sun.

Meanwhile my neck had gone to sleep from turning constantly towards Tsvetkov to give him the reaction he wanted, and I was lying awkwardly and uncomfortably: either Klygin hadn't covered me properly with the blanket or bits of my body had gone to sleep, and I felt as if some sort of grey mass was spreading inside me.

"They were redecorating the test room at the time, so Allochka used to sit in the library and Shipa, naturally, was hanging around there too. So they made this up about some books, and Shipa heaved a sigh as if he had been punched in the stomach and shot across the road, straight for her house. Vashakidze and Lang looked at each other and ran after him. They were just in time to grab him on the porch. They had to drag him back. Shipa didn't put up much resistance. I suppose he twigged they were having him on. He went sullen, called them sods. Lang showed him all about sods – took him into the dorm that evening and gave him a smack or two. Shipa sent all the bedside tables flying."

"Tsvetkov! Comrade junior sergeant," Klygin said in a tragic voice, putting his head through the door of the ward. "Go and mind the registration office, the nurse had to go off for a while. And make sure you stay there. Give our Correspondent a rest from your waffle."

I gave a few groans when Klygin took the cups off my back. Not so much from relief as because Klygin expected the groans and was pleased to hear them. "That's it," I thought. "I can have a sleep. How that wally pissed me off. Stories about a fool. What am I – a bucket for tipping rubbish into?"

But Klygin, having freed my back from captivity, dropped himself onto Tsvetkov's bed, rolled his eyes and sang:

"Oh, let me sleep, just an hour a day!"

He burst out laughing, dropping his eyes onto me as if he expected support.

I managed a faint smile.

"What has Tsvetkov been telling you?" he asked.

"About that… the one who was sleeping here… Shapovalenko, I think he's called."

"About Shipa? He's such a laugh, isn't he?"

Yes, I nodded, such a laugh. Very amusing and funny. A Fool is there to laugh at. You rub his face in the mud and he blows bubbles for you.

What fun! You can't help making fun of a rookie. Come here! Bring me demob! You don't understand? Bring me demob! I won't say it again. How d'you mean, "What am I supposed to do?" Go ask the rookies. They're all asleep? Wake them up! They don't know? OK, laddie, dad will explain, and you better get it right then. It's like this – when you hear the words, "Bring me demob", you have to go and get demob, nice and fast with no fuss. Got it? Bring me demob! Well? You're all confused? You were taking it easy, were you? You don't respect the dads. Then a punch in the chest or a smack in the face and off to the toilet and it better be spotless when I see it in the morning. It's an amusement park, the fun room. In your first year of service you are constantly guilty without guilt. In the second year you have fun and games. It's fair, fairer than a lot of things in life, where everything is mixed up: joy and sorrow. One side has all the joy, so much that it palls. The other side is a target for a lucky marksman – every shot's a bull's eye. Blind fate – it's unfair.

Here it's so much better. A year of pain and a year of happiness. Guaranteed. Except… Can it be proper happiness if it depends on someone else's pain? And can you be a proper person if you're set free after a year living with your own thoughts? Would that person really speak out after he'd been set free? Doesn't the slavish acceptance – you look on unconcerned as someone else is beaten up – get into your blood: thank God, it's not me, that's enough for life and happiness? When you know that the only person on your side is you.

Madness. That damned woodland glade, where my train has halted… where I want to shout to my good old fellow travellers, to my heart, my memory, my soul: "Get out! We've stopped! 'That' is all behind us for the moment. We can live out loud for a moment, breathe this air and look at the sky." But the glade doesn't come to life. The train stands there, an unwanted hulk, a child of movement, and the indifferent faces of the passengers are cold, grey and indistinct in the windows. We'll be on the move soon and the forest, calm and wrinkled, will be a wall once again and the clouds – trampolines for our hopes and dreams – will flash painfully and pointlessly past the window.

Madness. Is this really the first act, not the interval? What we saw in childhood was only costumes, the make-up room of goodness and light, sparing us the cruel play, where there is no God, and therefore no thread connecting events, connecting people, and no reward for good and no punishment for cruelty and evil. Is man really blind? Originally blind? Is this the real life? There, far away in the Eldorado of civilian life, is it really the same thing at bottom – just dressed up in nice clothes? God, it makes you dizzy... So this isn't the interval, a back room, but the road, the road along which we travel and travel... The damned hospital.

At lunch they give us porridge, and a lump of butter in the morning. Whatever happens we'll get butter in the morning, tasty and white. And in the evening I'll remember Ira, the tubby typist at the paper where I used to work, how I pawed her on the porch, groping insistently through her skirt, putting my sweaty fingers under her large-size T-shirt, and how she squeaked unpleasantly, not resisting but pressing her stiff, anxious body into mine still harder. When I come home my parents will give me an Alaska jacket and jeans. I'll earn a lot of money and build myself a house in the forest. Big and nice. And live in it alone. Alone. And no train whistle will reach my house. None at all. And I'll read detective stories and poetry. I'll throw out the TV set, and forget about all this. I had one caramel left in my bedside table. There were two, but I gave one to Tsvetkov. Fool. I could still eat the other one. It must have melted a bit, and I'd have to lick some of it off the wrapper. So long as Klygin doesn't look in the drawer – if he does he'll make sweet eyes and a funny face and I'll give him the caramel with a smile and even with a glad expression. When my father comes to visit he'll bring more. I hope he comes soon, like an ambassador from the country called "The Prologue", from where we are all emigrants.

So long as Klygin doesn't look in the bedside table.

Klygin has already spent ten minutes telling me about something, taking no notice of the blank expression on my face.

"Shipa was coming to the hospital every day. He was willing to come down with anything, so long as he could get a spell here. He kept asking me – get me in, get me in – thought I'd help him. Well, he got what he was asking for. He came out in a rash on his legs and backside – flaky sores. They sent him to us for ten days. We rubbed on disinfectant and the sores got a bit better. When he wasn't having treatment he spent his time cruising round the first floor, hoping to see Allochka if she came out of her room. He was like a dog at the door in winter: it's scared but eager to get in, so it rubs and rubs up against the door, then jumps back, and starts rubbing up again, whimpering. I had some fun with him… In the morning I need one person to go for the hospital rations. Of course you can't get anyone to wake up, they're not interested… But I always said to Shipa…" Klygin pulled a serious ingratiating face, "'Shurik'…" He couldn't stifle a laugh, but then he pulled a serious face again. "'Shurik, Allochka says hello', and he'd jump up and say, 'Really?!' with eyes

like cockades. I said, 'Really, of course.' After that he'd
come with me for the rations and wash the plates, good as
gold. But I got fed up with the blockhead after awhile –
me and Vanya Tsvetkov started knocking him about. Shipa
would be devouring some book, so he could take it back
to the library here as soon as possible, and get near to
Allochka… I'd sit down beside him and whisper: 'She's a
scrubber.' He wouldn't say anything, but I could see him
going red, and I'd say it again: 'She's a scrubber.' He'd
look up and snarl, 'Don't you dare say that!' Hissing at
me, his dad! And he'd go on: 'She is above that, and you
are disgusting.' How about that, eh?"

I nodded in full agreement.

"And he'd cover his snout with a pillow, so as not to
hear. Me and Tsvetkov sorted him out pretty quick: pinned
his arms and legs behind his back and yelled in each ear:
'Scrubber, she's a scrubber! She's done it with me, with
him, with him over there, with everyone, she's just a hole!'
Shipa twitched and croaked. Then he wouldn't talk to me
for a couple of days, but he soon got tired of cleaning the
toilet and he'd start sucking up to me again. Then one
day he had to quit in a hurry. The head doctor said on his
rounds that his sores were pretty much healed, and he
needed heat treatments. So he prescribed a five-day course.
Shipa ran after the doctor and asked to be let off the
treatment. But the doctor couldn't give a toss. 'Klygin,' he
said, 'make sure…' And Shipa hung his head. He kept
saying to me: my mum is going to send me three roubles

and I'll buy you a good feed. He kept ringing the company to find out if the money had come or not. Then he offered me his parade uniform: take it as a present, he said. I'll tell the sergeant I lost it. I laughed: they'll charge you for it! He thought for a minute and said, I'll write to my mum and she'll get the money for it. I'll pay her back after demob, every last kopek… What the hell did I want with his parade uniform – he's so thin, I couldn't get into it anyway. I grabbed him by the collar and laid it on the line: 'Listen, you turd on skis, you'll go skipping in for your treatment tomorrow, or I'll tell Allochka you're head over heels in love with her. Any questions, comrade lance-corporal?' He quietened down right away. I came over the next morning at six fifteen and he was already sitting up in bed, awake. He kept quiet all morning. I took him off after lunch. He came along with his teeth clenched, like he had a spike up his arse. I gave Allochka his papers and took him into the cabin. He lay down on his stomach. 'Pants off,' I told him, 'let's have a look at it'. He took them off reluctantly as if it were a huge effort. I gave him a slap on the thigh. 'There he is,' I said, 'our spotty leopard.' Allochka put down the heating light, screwed up her nose, and said: 'Don't go, deal with your patient yourself, please'. Shipa lay there quiet as a mouse all the ten minutes and then went straight to the head doctor. And the doctor discharged him. I thought he'd gone to sneak on me, but I haven't heard anything, so I still don't know what he was up to… So! Time to sleep? Sleep! Sleep! Sleep."

Before going to sleep I thought happily about how I'd be a dad one day – I'd go about with my shirt undone, in a leather belt and my boots creased. I'd be a tough dad and I'd learn how to talk to the rookies who'd be afraid of me and call me "beast". "What's up?" I'd say. "You don't understand the army, you little shit?! Get in that toilet. I'll be there in five minutes and I want to see my reflection in the wash basin!" I'd whack him in the stomach with my fist. So there are no bruises. Another three hundred days and I'll be a dad. A master.

In the morning I went for my electrophoresis. I felt gloomy. Either I hadn't slept well or it was the lack of light in winter that makes time pass more slowly.

"Correspondent! Correspondent, damn it..." It was Korobchik, a middler from our company, summoning me with his finger.

I went over to him, nearly choking with disgust, misery, and a sense of inevitability.

"What are we up to here? Shirking your army duty? On holiday?"

I looked at the end of my hospital slippers, with my hands loose at my sides.

"Nothing to say, laddie?"

"It's just that," I squeezed out an answer, "I've got pneumonia."

"What have you got?" Korobchik made a face.

"Chest cold. Pneumonia."

"Clever boy, uses long words - that's it, is it?!"

"No."

"How's the army treating you, eh?"

"Like a chicken."

"Why so slow to answer? Had a stroke?"

"I'm not slow."

"Why 'like a chicken'?"

"Wherever the cocks find me, they fu…"

"I'm waiting…"

"At least they don't kill me – I've got another day to look forward to."

"Louder."

"At least…"

"Ah-ha. Get well soon. We're missing you in the company – no one to clean the toilets."

I nearly managed a weak smile as if to say I don't mind cleaning toilets. But I hadn't got him on my side.

"What are you grinning at, pea-brain? Say 'I am a pea-brain'."

"I am a pea-brain."

"I'll bring you some work tomorrow. You're going to do my album. OK?"

"Yes."

"Off you go. We haven't whacked you often enough, But never mind – we'll make up for it."

My father is coming to see me soon. When I was little he cradled me on his knees, but now he's old and he sometimes cries when he comes to see me, though he tries not to let me see it. I cry too, and he sees that. At home, where he works, he's a boss. He has a lot of people under him. But he's finding it hard to do his job properly now. Because he often comes to see me.

He brings me home-made jam. Cherry jam. I like to chew the pits.

"Hello there."

"Hello…"

"Shall I sit here?"

And sausage. And apple pie in a plastic bag. And money. I tell him – don't bring money. But he still brings it. You can buy yourself something, he says. But the money gets borrowed. I don't tell him that – I lie to him about how I spend it. He brings me meatballs and liverwurst. He always brings loads to eat. I have a huge feast – I try to eat it all, so as not to take it back to the company. He sometimes eats with me: he's tired and hungry after the journey. But he doesn't eat much. Just nibbles. As if he's shy about eating too much.

"Lie down, why are you sitting?"

My father told me I had grown up…

"This will be prickly."

No, pa, I haven't grown up, I've grown old.

"Why doesn't that baldpate come for treatment?"

Old people are children too, but they're weak and foolish…

"So why doesn't the baldy come?"

"He's not bald," I said under my nose. But then I raised myself up on one elbow and shouted:

"He's not bald," the metal strips on my chest didn't slip. I only saw her back.

"What," she said, writing something down.

I sat right up. The strips fell on the floor. I looked around: what could I do with the ringing, itching tremble in my hands and my soul? I pushed a flowerpot. It rocked a little and settled. The couch was warm and I wanted to lie down again.

"He's not bald!" I shouted and pushed the pot as hard as I could. My hand slipped, but the pot fell, spilling a tongue of earth on the linoleum. The white spot of her face turned colourful and a sharp female voice rasped: "What on earth are you doing?"

I got up and walked, then ran, overwhelmed with that damned black tremble. I pulled a curtain from the door, knocked some test tubes off the table and ran out into the corridor, not seeing myself in the mirror. I ran as fast as I could…Then there were some hands emerging from a huge palpitating wave and someone's voice in front of the wave, which was about to engulf me:

"So young and so nervous… What were you before the army?"

With a last effort I said:

"A human being."

THE GENERAL

…The miraculous title, which means something quite different in Russia from what it means, for example, well… well there, where things aren't like they are here… only in Russia are the distances between lieutenant-colonel and colonel, and between colonel and general, as incomparable as the distances between your nostrils and between Mars and Earth. If you are a general you can speak to everyone in familiar terms, you change your walk, you're never again seen hurrying along a corridor. You do not stand in queues or travel by bus. If you make a joke everyone laughs assiduously. If you look into an office, everyone freezes. Legends and anecdotes are told about you. It's your sacred right to have eccentricities, to communicate in cow-like interjections and epileptic gestures, which leave subordinates desperately guessing what you could have meant. Your subordinates adjust their work routine to yours and each of them tries to pass you in the corridor late in the evening with a careworn and honest expression, hoping to be noticed as a straight-forward, honest officer.

You like to be on the level with the soldiers, so you stop a terrified private you happen to meet and ask him, folding your face into lines: "Well, er, how's the army treating you?"

And the soldier, with bright eyes bulging, reels off an answer in a voice that half the garrison can hear, ending with the refrain "Com-rade Gen-er-al..." And your officers smile touchingly behind your back, as if to say, "He's like a father to them."

You have a red-haired adjutant, who puts the fear of God into everyone and fears only you. The adjutant is a little copy of you, curses like you, knits his brows like you, and when the adjutant says, "I'll report back," the silence is total. All your subordinates use the same expressions as you when they are angry, from the chief of staff to the last soldier.

But your most sacred right is to shout at people – broadening your shoulders, throwing back you head, turning your eyes into drills, revelling in it. It's your right to shout till eardrums ring, your mouth contorted with disgust, till the faces around you are deathly white, confirming the distance between you and everyone else. "Look at the mess you clowns have made here, and I have to answer for it, I have to face the music!" To shout till you are blue in the face and foaming at the mouth, personifying fate, as if blotting out the existence of other people from you memory, forever and irreversibly – to shout and to shout!

What a thing to be a general – everyone else must smile at you: your subordinates, your wife, the waitress, the adjutant, even passers-by, while you can do as you please. You can be happy or you can be out of sorts, because you are YOU!

You may not be God, but you are his golden, indisputable, marvellous reflection on this earth!

ON THE TRAIN

"What's the time?"

"Half past one. Rostov soon… 12-minute stop."

"We'll have a smoke there and then hit the hay. I'll get dressed now so I'm ready, OK?"

"What's with the striped vest. You in the commandos?"

"'Course I am."

"My brother is too. Yeah! He told me how their battalion commander taught the young ones to jump. The commander came to the aerodrome and they called out the ones who'd refused to jump the first and second time. He said to them: 'To hell with you. We won't try jumping today – why make you suffer for nothing? Just pack your parachutes and go for a ride – at least get used to the plane.' And he winked to the flight engineer. So the soldiers got ready, strapped on their parachutes and up they went. After about twenty minutes the flight engineer lit a smoke grenade on the quiet, threw it in the cabin and screamed 'Fire!' They ran for the exit so fast they nearly pushed out the man at the hatch!"

"That's a good way, but our battalion commander wouldn't think of it. He was as thick as two planks, but always trying tricks, thought he was smart. Once on manoeuvres the engineers were looking the wrong way, and two hundred litres of spirit disappeared, as if by magic. What could they do? No one had seen anything – who, when, who'd helped to do it. The major called me in. I was a pretty big prick in the Komsomol. He says: 'So what are we going to do about this theft incident?' I say, 'I don't know.' What was it to me – I hadn't drunk the stuff… 'Right,' he says, 'I'll tell you how to catch them out. Line them up tomorrow and say there's been a terrible coincidence. That spirit had already been used in planes. Irreversible changes begin in the body two days after ingestion. Tell them the doctor says that death is certain in eight cases out of ten. Anonymous special visits to the clinic start immediately after parade – everyone who drank that spirit must have an injection by five this evening. In view of the gravity of the situation there'll be no disciplinary action. That's what you'll say, and not a word about our conversation to anyone.' I didn't say a word. What was it to me? I hadn't tasted the stuff. I gave them the speech at parade. Do you think any of them came to see the doctor? Not a soul!"

"We had a sergeant major who was one for searches. Before New Year's Eve the lads brought two bottles of vodka, and we rushed to find a hiding place. We poured it into a water canister, nice and proper. The sergeant turned up on the thirtieth and started rummaging. He went through everything – no luck. He went through it all a second time: 'The second battery can't be without vodka at New Year. It just can't be.' He searched and searched, and we all stood stiff to attention, wouldn't move a muscle. He got all sweaty and asked where the water was. We hung our heads. He tipped a cupful from the canister, took a gulp, gave us a wild look, drank off the rest, slammed down the cup and shot out of the cabin. We thought – that's it, he'll be back to give us what for, but no, not a bit of it. He didn't come back."

"Right, and what's this? Rostov?"

"Looks like it. Coming for a smoke?"

FEAR OF FROST

Railway stations are the crossroads of our lives, where we abandon our well-worn ruts and intersect with a multitude of other people. We become exposed there to all the circumstances that make the essence of these crossroads – be they railway stations, hospitals, stores, laundries, canteens, airports, or communal toilets. They are always a test of a society's ability to think and to act. They are indicators of its lung function. Arrive by night at a railway station or an airport, and you will hear how wheezy, how laboured is our breathing, how we sigh, how we choke on clots of blood. Night decants its sediment, and it is terrible.

Here waiting passengers are sleeping right on the floor. The fortunate few are huddled along the walls while latecomers make do with a pitch across a passageway. They are uneasy, ashamed at the outset, but fatigue erases their feelings, wipes the creases of expression from their faces, and crumples any trace of bearing. They all sleep the same sleep, indiscriminate, heavy and shameful.

The people sleep, leaning shoulder to shoulder, their

defenseless, childlike faces painful to behold. Husbands embrace their wives awkwardly, ashamed of exhibiting in public this ordinary, intimate gesture. Mothers shield their children between themselves and the wall. The children sleep with pale, frightened faces, tense against the stuffiness and the heat. They sleep on newspapers, bags and boxes, on the bare, soiled floor. Here's a one-legged man sleeping with his head leaning against a seat.

In this world, expensive fur jackets jostle with soldiers' greatcoats, felt boots with army jackboots, children's overcoats with leather jerkins, and fur hats are of all descriptions. There are workingmen asleep here, and doctors and schoolchildren, officers, teachers and managers. This is equality. This is the lowest common denominator of the barracks, the easiest one of all to achieve.

We have grown used to being patient. History has taught us discipline. But today, when bread has long been unrationed, when class enemies no longer breathe so hotly down our necks, from whence derives this universal submissiveness, our so easily depreciated sense of human dignity?

The man who sleeps on the railway station floor and also suffers his daily dose of torture in the queues is a daily witness to filth and rudeness. He will never feel like watching a full-length television documentary, never dream of owning a factory, never read the biography of a parliamentary candidate, and will never, ever, give shelter to his neighbour. Who ever gave a shelter to him?

It is shameful that we only become human beings in times of flood or fire or war. Can only tragedy make us raise our heads?

Where did our self-respect go, and why did it leave us all at the same time? We have all lost it, not only the man sleeping on the filthy tiles of the station floor but the station managers too. I do not believe that, just in order for people to relate to each other decently, we have to start with billions of roubles, or with reliable suppliers of goods. Before all else, we need some sense of human dignity, common to all of us, independent of the "system", with its roots in self-respect.

Do people who manufacture sophisticated cameras, computers, yachts, space stations, marble memorials and granite riverside drives have to suffer in inhuman conditions waiting for a train or a plane in station buildings where there is no room to move for the bodies lying on the floor?

It was in the army that I first became aware of the lack of self-respect. I understood then that I lacked something that would have enabled me to call myself a human being. It was easy to humiliate me. The entire army system of relationships beyond the military manual – like fagging in a public school – is built on daily humiliation, both physical and moral which amounts to savagery. Serving in an elite unit, I had no right for a year to wash morning and evening, to go to the library or to watch television. The first time I was stripped and beaten in the toilets, it was because, watching the news, the only program allowed, I had seated myself slightly apart from the lads in my draft.

In the army, I understood that there is not enough justice to go round. They invent their own justice in the army. They model our society after their own fashion: one group crushes another. In order to survive, you have to crush someone else. This does not end with your release from the army.

Moral losses are like radiation, colourless and odourless, and the more terrifying for that. The man who has been treated as a non-person finds it very easy to live afterwards. It sets my very teeth on edge when I hear the words "The army is a good school of life" – it's true!

Until my army service, I had hated the endless food queues, been exasperated by the formalities of production meetings, and my spirit yearned for something it lacked. But after the army I became quite reconciled. I saw, and still see all around me, the ingrained humiliations of the army. Yet how little we all need for our happiness! Never mind the queues and the rude salesgirls – we've bought something, haven't we? Never mind if we sleep on the floor – we're travelling, aren't we? Even if it's without a seat, in an unheated compartment – we're going home! Never mind if the boss curses – at least he's not beating us! Never mind if the toilet's filthy – it's still better than doing it in the bushes.

The army is not responsible for what goes into the

psychology of relationships beyond the military manual. It is no paradox – and it certainly won't soften the *dedovschina* system – that a man, humiliated for an entire year, will subsequently humiliate and beat in his turn. The more fiercely, the more he has been beaten himself.

I first saw a man die with my own eyes at a quiet little railway station. The stationmaster had twice announced the departure platform incorrectly. There were frequent duplications in the reservations, condemning people to act according to the savage principle of "finders, keepers". The passengers therefore, and among them this particular ex-serviceman, rushed over the bridge from platform to platform to meet the long-awaited train. This man was lucky: he reached his carriage first and, breathing heavily, began to shove his way towards his compartment, hanging on for dear life to his two suitcases, which he needed in order to grab two extra seats, for his wife and daughter. He wanted them at least to be able to sit down, even if there was not enough room to lie down. The man's heart gave out in the narrow corridor, and he fell face down. The other passengers, huffing and puffing, clambered over his body, passing bags and boxes, hurrying to secure their places.

When everyone had found a seat, they eventually carried the man out on to the platform, where his daughter gave him artificial respiration. She did it expertly – he must have suffered from heart trouble – but she could not save him. He had just wanted to secure his place on the delayed train. Our way of life gave him no choice. The daughter was groaning pitiably for breath, pressing rhythmically on the man's ribcage. In her hands was the life of her father who in childhood had seemed immortal and whose face now, on the grey asphalt, after a happy vacation, had become strange and dreadful. People stood around, the carriage attendant looked out – wasn't the signal green yet? The passengers craned out of the windows. The man died.

They carried his suitcases on to the platform, and the train pulled out.

ROSSICA TRANSLATION PRIZE

The Winner

ON 24 MAY 2007, ACADEMIA ROSSICA AND THE YELTSIN
FOUNDATION ANNOUNCED THE WINNER OF THE ROSSICA
TRANSLATION PRIZE WHICH WENT TO JOANNE TURNBULL,
TRANSLATOR OF *7 STORIES* BY SIGIZMUND KRZHIZHANOVSKY, AND
TO GLAS PUBLISHERS.

The judges' verdict:

*"In the face of strong competition, we believe that the prize
should go to Joanne Turnbull for the resourcefulness and verve
with which she has introduced to English speakers the
extraordinarily inventive and linguistically challenging work
of Sigizmund Krzhizhanovsky, 'a writer-visionary, an unsung
genius' who died in obscurity in 1950 but since 1989 has
begun to be recognised by Russians as one of their great prose
writers of the 20th century."*

The posthumous publication of Krzhizhanovsky's work,
who described himself as "known for being unknown",
confirmed the writer's belief that his reader would come in
fifty years' time. His work, including *7 **Stories***, of which
only two were published during his lifetime, now for the
first time **translated into English by Joanne Turnbull**, is said
to have changed the face of 20th century Russian letters.

Elaine Feinstein, writer, literary critic and one of the
Rossica Prize judges, says: *"What is astonishing is not that
he was 'known for being unknown', but that his genius survived
Soviet disapproval to be rediscovered long after his death."*

Written between 1922 and 1939, these remarkable

stories attest to Krzhizhanovsky's boundless imagination, black humour and breathtaking irony. A man loses his way in the vast black waste of his own small room. A woman's former lovers wind up confined to the recesses of her pupil. The rebellious hand of a famous pianist flees a concert hall in mid-performance. Another man lives to try and bite his own elbow. A bibliophile finds that he has lost his 'I' in the new Soviet order. A scientist solves the energy crisis by converting human spite. The Eiffel Tower goes mad and drowns itself in Lake Constance...

Special Commendation

The judges of the 2007 Rossica Prize gave a Special Commendation to **Robert Chandler** for his translation of *The Railway* by Hamid Ismailov (Harvill Secker) in recognition both of the merits of this particular rendition, and of the excellent work that he has done over the years in bringing Russian literature to the English reader.

Chandler was also short-listed for the 2005 Rossica Prize for his translation of *Soul* by Andrey Platonov, for which he won the American Association of Teachers of Slavic and East European Languages award for best translation from a Slavonic language. Chandler is particularly known for his translations of Platonov which include *The Portable Platonov* published by Glas.

The Jury

The judges for the **2007 Rossica Translation Prize** were: Elaine Feinstein, writer and literary critic; Peter France, Professor Emeritus, University of Edinburgh; and Catriona Kelly, Professor of Russian at the University of Oxford.

ROSSICA TRANSLATION PRIZE

7 STORIES
by Sigizmund Krzhizhanovsky
translated by Joanne Turnbull
wins the 2007
Rossica Translation Prize
for excellence in literary translation from
Russian into English

Publishers wishing to enter books for the **2009**
Rossica Translation Prize should contact Academia Rossica
on +44 207 937 5001 or rossica@academia-rossica.org
Deadline for submissions 31 December 2008.

Academia Rossica, established in 2000, is a London-based arts
organisation promoting Russian culture and cultural links
between Russia and the West. With its many varied projects AR
looks to advance the understanding and awareness of Russian
culture internationally. One of AR's many exciting projects is
the Rossica Translation Prize, set up in 2004, and awarded for
the first time in 2005. In 2008, AR plans to publish a selection
of contemporary Russian writing in translation before awarding
the next Rossica Prize in 2009.